Guy Newell Boothby

Sheilah McLeod

A hHeroine of the Back Blocks

Guy Newell Boothby

Sheilah McLeod
A hHeroine of the Back Blocks

ISBN/EAN: 9783337189105

Printed in Europe, USA, Canada, Australia, Japan

Cover: Foto ©Andreas Hilbeck / pixelio.de

More available books at **www.hansebooks.com**

SHEILAH McLEOD

A Heroine of the Back Blocks

BY

GUY BOOTHBY

AUTHOR OF

'DR NIKOLA,' 'A BID FOR FORTUNE,' 'THE BEAUTIFUL WHITE
DEVIL,' 'THE FASCINATION OF THE KING,' ETC.

LONDON

SKEFFINGTON & SON, PICCADILLY

Publishers to H.M. The Queen and to H.R.H. The Prince of Wales

1897

All Rights reserved.

CONTENTS

SHEILAH McLEOD

PROLOGUE

VAKALAVI IN THE SAMOAN GROUP

LOOKING back on it now I can recall every circumstance connected with that day just as plainly as if it had all happened but yesterday. In the first place, it was about the middle of the afternoon, and the S.E. trade, which had been blowing lustily since ten o'clock, was beginning to die away according to custom.

There had been a slight shower of rain in the forenoon, and now, standing in the verandah of my station looking across the blue lagoon with its fringe of boiling surf, it was my good fortune not only to have before me one of the finest pictures in the South Pacific, but to be able to distinctly smell the sweet perfume of the frangipani blossom and wild lime in the jungle which clothed the hillside behind me. I walked to one end

A

of the verandah and stood watching a group of native girls making tappa outside the nearest hut—then to the other, and glanced into my overflowing copra shed, and from it at the bare shelves of the big trade room opposite. The one, as I say, was full, the other sadly empty, and for more than a week I had been bitterly lamenting the non-arrival of the company's schooner, which was supposed to visit the island once every six months in order to remove my gains and to supply me with sufficient trade to carry me safely through the next half-year.   The schooner was now ten days overdue, and I had made sure she would put in an appearance that morning; but the wind was failing, and it was, therefore, ten chances to one against our seeing her before the next forenoon.   I was more than a little disappointed, if only on the score of the company I should have had, for you must understand that it was nearly six months since I had seen a white face, and even then the face was only that of a missionary.   But, in common fairness, I must confess that that missionary was as different to the usual run of his cloth as chalk is to cheese—a good fellow in every way, not a bit bumptious, or la-di-dardy, or fond of coming the Oxford scholar-

and-a-gentleman touch, but a real white man from top to toe. And my first meeting with him was as extraordinary as anyone could imagine, or wish for. It's a yarn against myself, but as it shows you what queer beasts we men are, I may as well tell you about it. It happened in this way :—

About ten o'clock one fine spring morning I was coming down the hillside behind my house, and, according to custom, pulled up at the Big Plateau and looked out to sea. To the north and south nothing was in sight, but to the eastward there was a tiny blotch on the horizon which gradually developed into a small fore-and-aft schooner of about fifty tons. When she was level with the island she worked steadily up the reef until she found the passage through the surf; then, having edged her way into the lagoon, came to an anchor opposite my house. Seeing that she was going to send a boat ashore, and suspecting some sort of missionary mischief from the cut of her jib, down I went to the beach and got ready to receive her.

The craft she was sending ashore was a double-ended surf boat, and a well-built one at that, pulled by two Solomon boys, and steered by a white man in a queer kind of helmet that I believe they call a 'solar topee' in India. The man in the helmet brought her up in first-class style, and was preparing to beach her just in front of where I stood when I held up my hand in warning.

'Who are you, and what do you want here?' I asked, looking him up and down.

'I'm the new missionary at Futuleima,' says he, as bold as brass, 'and as I had a couple of spare days at my disposal I thought I would come across and talk to the people on this island. Have you anything to say against it?'

'Not much,' I answered, feeling my dander rising at the cool way in which he addressed me, 'but what I *do* say I mean.'

'And what is it you mean, my friend?' he asked.

'I mean that you don't set foot ashore if I can prevent it,' I replied. 'You understand me once and for all. I'm the boss of this island, and I'm not going to have any of your nonsense talked to my men. I'm civilising 'em on my own lines, and I won't have you inter- fering and shoving your nose in where it ain't wanted.'

'I'm afraid you speak your mind with more candour than courtesy,' he said, mopping his

forehead with a snow-white pocket-handkerchief which he had taken from his pocket.

'You think so, do you?' I cried. 'Well, you
just set as much as your little toe on this beach
and you'll see that I mean it!'

'So I'm to choose between fighting you and
going away with my errand unaccomplished?'
he answered, still as cool as a cucumber. 'Do
I take you properly?'

'That is my meaning, and I reckon it's a
bigger one than you can digest,' I replied, like
the hot-tempered fool I was. 'Let me tell
you, you're not the first of your breed that has
tasted my fist and gone away with his appetite
satisfied.'

'Then since it is to be the Church Militant
here on Earth, and there's no other way out of
it, I suppose I must agree to your proposal,' he
said, after a moment's thought, and forthwith
jumped out of the boat on to the beach. 'But
let it be somewhere where my boatmen cannot
see. I don't know that the example would be
altogether beneficial to them.'

As he stood on the beach before me, Heaven
knows it was a poor enough figure of a man he
made. He was not as big as me by a head and
a half; for I stand close on six feet in my socks,
and am bigger in the beam than the ordinary

run of men ; besides which, I am always, of necessity, in the pink of condition. To think, therefore, that such a little whipper - snapper should contemplate fighting me was too absurd. I stood and stared at him.

'You don't mean to say you intend to put your fists up ?' I cried, letting him see how astonished I was.

'That I do !' he said, and bidding his men wait for him he led the way up the path to the jungle at the back of the station house. 'Since you deem it necessary that I should introduce myself to you in such a strange fashion, I feel it incumbent upon me to do so. Besides, I want to teach you a lesson you will not forget.' Then, stopping short in his walk, he felt the muscle of my right arm critically and smiled. 'You'll be a man worth fighting,' he said, and continued his walk.

Well, here I was in a mighty curious position, as you will understand. Having seen the plucky way he had jumped ashore and taken me up, right in my teeth, so to speak, I felt I had made a precious fool of myself in being so ready with my challenge. He was a man and not a monkey, like most of his fraternity, and he might have converted every nigger in the South Pacific for all I should have cared. I wouldn't have stopped a man like him for all the world, for I reckon he wouldn't have taught 'em anything shady for the life of him. But there was no hope for it now, so I walked up the path beside him, as meek as a new-born lamb, till we came to an open patch at the base of a small waterfall.

'This should suit our purpose, I think,' he said, taking off his helmet and coat and placing them beneath a tree. 'If you're quite ready, let us get to business.'

'Hold on,' I cried, 'this won't do. I've changed my mind, and I'm not going to fight you after all! Missionary or no missionary, you're a man, and a proper sort of man too; and what's more, you shall waltz every nigger on this island backwards and forwards in and out of Purgatory as often as you please, for all I'll say you nay.'

'That's very kind of you,' he answered, at the same time looking me in the face in a curious sort of fashion. 'Nevertheless, for the good of your own soul, I intend that you shall fight me, and at once.'

'I won't, and that's the end of it,' I said.

'You will, and immediately,' he answered quietly. Then, walking up to me, he drew back his arm and hit me a blow in the face. For a

second I was too much surprised to do anything at all, but, recovering myself, I lifted
my fist and drove it home under his jaw. He
went down like a ninepin and rolled almost
over, but before I could say 'knife' he was up
and at me again. After that I didn't stop to
consider, but just let him have it, straight from
the shoulder, as fast as he could take it.
Take it he did, like a glutton, and asked for
more, but it was sickening work for all that,
and though I did my best to give him satis-
faction, I found I could put no heart in it.

When I had sent him flying head over
heels in the grass for the sixth time, and his
face was a good deal more like an underdone
beefsteak than anything else, I could stand
it no longer, and I told him so. But it made
no difference; he got on to his feet and ran
at me again, this time catching me a good one
on the left jaw. In sheer self-defence I had
to send him down, though I loathed myself
as a beast of the worst kind for doing it. But
even then he was not satisfied. Once more
he came in at me and once more I had to
let him have it. By this time he could hardly
see out of his eyes, and his face was streaming with blood.

'That's enough,' I cried, 'I'll have no more

of it.   I'm a big bully, and you're the best plucked little fellow this side of Kingdom Come!   I'll not lay another finger on you, even if you knock me into a jelly trying to make me.   Get up and shake hands.'

He got on to his feet and held out his hand.

'All things considered, this is the queerest bit of proselytizing I have ever done,' he said. 'But somehow I think I've taught you a lesson, my friend!'

'You have,' I answered, humbly, 'and one that I'll never forget if I live to be a hundred. I deserve to be kicked.'

'No!   You're a man, and a better man, if I'm not mistaken, than you were half-an-hour ago.'

He said no more on the subject then, but went over to the little pool below the waterfall and bathed his face.   I can tell you I felt pretty rocky and mean as I watched him. And any man who knows my reputation among the Islands will tell you that's a big admission for Jim Heggarstone to make.

After that he stayed with me until his bruises disappeared; and when he went away I had made a firm friend of him, and told him all the queer story that I have set myself to tell you in this book.   Ever since that time he's been one of my staunchest and truest pals on earth, and all I can say is if there's any man has got a word to say against the Rev. William Carson-Otway, he had better not say it in my hearing—that's all.

But in telling you all this I've been wandering off my course, and now I must get back to the afternoon of the day when I was awaiting the arrival of the schooner *Wildfowl* with a cargo of trade from Apia. As I have told you the wind had almost dropped, and for that reason I had given up all hope of seeing anything of her before morning. But, as it happened, I was mistaken, for just about sundown she hove in sight, rounded the bit of headland that sheltered the bay on the eastern side, and, having safely made the passage, brought up in the lagoon. Her arrival put me in the best of spirits, for after all those months spent alone with natives, I was fairly sick for a talk with a white man again. Long before her anchor was down I was on the beach getting my boat into the water, and by the time the rattle of the cable in the hawse-hole had died away, I was alongside and clambering aboard. I shook hands with the skipper, who was standing aft near the deck-house, then glanced at another

man whose back was towards me. By-and-
by he swung round and looked me in the face.
Then I saw that it was Dan Nicholson of Sal-
fulga Island, on the other side—the biggest
blackguard and bully in the Pacific, and I don't
care where you look for the next. An ugly
smile came over his face as he recognised me,
and then he said very politely,—

'And pray how do we find our dear friend,
the Rev. James Heggarstone, to-day?'

'None the better for seeing your face, Dan
Nicholson,' I answered sharply. 'And now
since you're here I'll give you a bit of advice.
Don't you set your foot ashore while this
boat's at anchor, or, as sure as you're born,
I'll teach you a lesson you'll not forget as
long as you live.'

'As you did that poor, soft-headed Futuleima
missionary cuss, I suppose,' he answered, turning a bit red and shifting uneasily on his feet.
'Well, having something else on hand just
now, I don't think I'll trouble you this time,
beloved brother.'

I saw that he had taken the hint, so I could
afford to forgive the way he spoke.

After a bit more palaver I got my budget
of letters, which I put into my pyjama pocket,
and then, accompanied by the skipper and

supercargo, went ashore. We strolled up to the station together, and while they sat and smoked in the verandah I hunted up some food and set it before them, with the last two bottles of gin I had in the store. I am a strict teetotaler myself, and have been ever since the events I have set myself to tell you about occurred. It was mainly the drink that did that bit of mischief, and for the same reason—but there, whatever the reasons may have been, I don't see that I need bother you with them till they come into the story in their proper places. This yarn is not a temperance tract, is it?

While they were at their meal I wandered outside to look through my mail. Two of the letters were from the trading firm I represented at Vakalavi. One was from Otway the missionary, warning me of an intended visit, another was a circular from an Apia storekeeper, enclosing a list of things a man in my situation could never possibly require; but the fifth was altogether different, and brought me up all standing, as the sailors say. With trembling hands, and a face as white as the bit of paper I'm now writing on, I opened it and read it through. Then the whole world seemed suddenly to change for me.

The sun of my life came out from behind the cloud that had covered it for so long, and, big, rough man as I was, I leaned my back against the wall behind me, feeling fairly sick with thankfulness. What a moment that was! I could have gone out and shouted my joy aloud to the world. The one thing of all others that I had longed for with my whole heart and soul had come at last.

I remained where I was for a while, thinking and thinking, but at the end of half-an-hour, having got my feelings under some sort of control, I went back to the verandah, where I found my guests smoking their pipes. Then we sat talking of mutual friends and common experiences for something like an hour, myself with a greater happiness in my heart than I had ever felt in my life before.

Living as I had lived for so long, the only white man on the island, with never a chance of hearing from or of my old Australian world, it may not be a matter for surprise that I had many questions to ask, and much news to hear. Since the schooner had last come my way great changes had occurred in the world, and on each I had to be rightly and exhaustively informed. The skipper and supercargo were both fluent talkers, and only too eager to tell me everything, so I had nothing to do but to lie back in my chair and listen.

Suddenly, in the middle of the narrative, a woman's scream rang out on the night air. Before it had finished I had jumped to my feet and run into the house, to return a moment later with a Winchester and a handful of cartridges.

'For God's sake, man, what are you going to do?' shouted the skipper, seeing the look upon my face, as I opened the magazine of the rifle and jammed the cartridges in.

'I'm going to find out what that scream meant,' I answered, as I turned towards the verandah steps.

'Be careful what you're up to with that rifle,' he said. 'Remember two can play at that game.'

'You bet your life,' I replied, and ran down the steps and along the path towards the bit of jungle on the left of the house.

Out on the open it was all quiet as death, and I knew exactly why. I entered the thicket pretty cautiously, and before I had gone ten yards discovered what I had expected to find there. It was Dan Nicholson sure enough, and one glance showed me that he held in his arms buxom little Faauma, the daughter

of Salevao, the head man of the island. By
the way he was standing, I could tell that she
had been struggling, and, from the tilt of his
right arm, I guessed that his fingers were
on her throat, and that he was threatening
to choke her if she uttered another sound. I
moved out of the undergrowth and took stock
of him.

'So this is the way you attend to my instructions, is it, Mr Nicholson?' I said, kicking
a bit of dead wood out of the way, and
bringing my rifle to the port in case of
mischief. 'Look here, I don't want to shoot
you on my own grounds, when you're, so to
speak, my guest, but, by God, if you don't
put those hands of yours up above your head
and right-about-face for the beach this very instant, I swear I'll drill you through and through
as sure as you're born. You understand me
now; I've got nine deaths under my finger,
and all of 'em waiting to look into your car-
case, so, if you turn round as much as an inch,
you're booked for Kingdom Come.'

He never said a word, but dropped the girl
right there, and put his hands up as I had
ordered him.

'That's right, I said. 'Now march.'

Without a word he turned to the rightabouts

and set off through the scrub for the beach.
I followed behind him, with the rifle on my
arm ready to come to the shoulder at an
instant's notice. The surf rolled upon the
reef like distant thunder, the stars shone
down upon the still lagoon, and through the
palm-leaves I could just discern the outline
of the schooner.

'Now, sir,' I said, when we arrived at the
water's edge, 'I'll have to trouble you to
swim out to yonder vessel. Don't say no,
or dare to turn round; for if you disobey me,
you're dead pig that instant.'

'But I can't swim,' he cried, grinding his
teeth so savagely that I could hear him yards
away.

'That be hanged for a yarn,' I said quietly.
'You swam well enough the day Big-head
Brown fired you off his lugger at Apia.
Come, in you go, and no more palaver, or
you and I will quarrel.'

'But I shall be eaten by sharks,' he cried,
this time meaning what he said very
thoroughly.

'And I wish them joy of a dashed poor
meal,' I answered. 'Come, in you go!'

With that he began to blubber outright
like a great baby, and while he was doing

so I couldn't help thinking what a strange
situation it was. Picture for yourself two
men, with the starlit heavens looking down
on them, standing on the edge of a big
lagoon, one talking and the other blubbering
like a baby that's afraid of the water. I
was about tired of it by this time, so I gave
him two minutes in which to make up his
mind, and promised him, in the event of
his not deciding to strike out then, that I'd
fire. Consequently he waded in without
more ado, and when I had seen him more
than half way out to the schooner, I put
the rifle under my arm and went back to
the house.

My guests had evidently been listening
to our conversation, and at the same time
amusing themselves with my gin bottles.

'You seem to have turned mighty strait-
laced all of a sudden, Mr Heggarstone,'
said the skipper, a little coldly as I came
up the steps and stood the rifle in a corner.

'You think so, do you?' I answered.
'And why so, pray?'

'It was only a native girl at the best
calculation,' said he. 'And, in my opinion,
she ought to think herself mighty well
honoured to be taken notice of. She ain't

a European queen or an extra special female martyr, is she?'

'I reckon she's a woman, anyhow,' I replied. 'And no Nicholson that ever was born, or any other living man for the matter of that, is big enough to play fast and loose with the women of my island while I'm about! So don't you make any mistake about that, my friend.'

'You seem to think a precious deal more of the sex on your patch than we do down our way,' says he.

'Perhaps so! And what if I do?'

'Nothing, of course, but I don't know that it's a good idea to side with the niggers against white men. That's all,' he continued, looking a trifle foolish, as he saw the way I was staring at him.

'Don't you? Well, when you've had sufficient experience, perhaps you'll think differently. No, sirree, I tell you that the man who says a word against a woman, black or white, in my hearing has to go down, and I don't care who he is.'

'Of course, you've a right to your own opinions,' he answered.

'I have, and what's more, I think I'm big enough to back them!'

The supercargo, all this time, had sat as quiet as a mouse.   Now he put his spoke into the conversation.

'I suppose there's a yarn at the back of all this palaver.'

'There is,' I answered, 'and a mighty big one too.   What's more, if you like, you shall hear it.   And then, when I've done, if it don't make you swear a woman's just the noblest and sweetest work of God's right hand, and that the majority of men ain't fit to tie her shoe laces, well, then, all I can say is you're not the fellows I take you to be.'

'Give me a light for my pipe,' the skipper said, 'and after that fire away.   I like a yarn first-rate.   The night's young, this bottle's about half-full, and if it takes till morning, well, you'll find I'm not the chap to grumble.'

I furnished him with a box of matches, and then, seating myself in a long cane chair beside the verandah rails, lit my pipe and began the yarn which constitutes this book.

CHAPTER I

OLD BARRANDA ON THE CARGOO RIVER, SOUTH-WESTERN QUEENSLAND

WHEN first I remember old Barranda Township on the Cargoo River, South - Western Queensland, it was not what it is to-day. There were no grand three-storeyed hotels, with gilded and mirror-hung saloons, and pretty, bright-eyed barmaids, in the main street then; no macadamised roads, no smart villa residences peeping from groves of Moreton Bay fig-trees and stretching for more than a mile out into the country on either side, no gas lamps, no theatre, no School of Arts, no churches or chapels, no Squatters' Club, and, above all, no railway line connecting it with Brisbane and the outer world. No! There were none of these things. The township, however, lay down in the long gully, beside the winding, ugly creek just as it does to-day—but in those days its site was only a clearing out of the primeval bush; the houses were, to use an Irishism, either tents or slab huts; two hotels certainly graced the main street, but they were grog shanties of the most villainous description, and were only patronised by the riff-raff of the country side. The only means of communicating with the metropolis was by the bullock waggons that brought up our stores once every six months, or by riding to the nearest township, one hundred and eight miles distant, and taking the coach from there—a long and wearisome journey that few cared to undertake.

One thing has always puzzled me, and that was how it came about that my father ever settled on the Cargoo. Whatever his reason may have been, however, certain was it that he was one of the earliest to reach the river, a fact which was demonstrated by the significant circumstance that he held possession of the finest site for a house and the pick of all the best country for miles around the township. It was in the earliest days that he made his way out west, and if I have my suspicions of why he came to Australia at all, well, I have always kept them religiously to myself, and intend to go on doing so. But before I say anything about my father, let me tell you what I remember of the old home.

It stood, as I suppose it does to-day, for it is many years since I set eyes on it, on a sort of small tableland or plateau on the hillside, a matter of a hundred yards above the creek, and at just the one spot where it could command a lovely view down the gully and across the roofs of the township towards the distant hills. It was a well-built place of six rooms, constructed of pisa, the only house of that description in the township—and, for that matter, I believe, in the whole district. A broad verandah, covered with the beautiful Wisteria creeper, ran all round it; in front was a large flower garden stretching away to the ford, filled with such plants and shrubs as will grow out in that country; to the right was the horse and cow paddock; and, on the left, the bit of cultivation we always kept going for the summer months, when green food is as valuable as a deposit at the bank. At the rear was another strip of garden with some fine orange and loquot trees, and then, on the other side of the stockyard rails, the thick scrub running up the hillside and extending for miles into the back country. The interior of the house was comfortably furnished, in a style the like of which I have never seen anywhere else in the Bush. I have a faint recollection of hearing that the greater part of it—the chairs, tables, pictures, book-cases and silver — came out from England the year that I was born, and were part of some property my father had inherited. But how much truth there was in this I cannot say. At anyrate, I can remember those chairs distinctly; they were big and curiously shaped, carved all over with a pattern having fruit in it, and each one had a hand clasping a battle-axe on a lozenge on the back—a crest I suppose it must have been, but whose I never took the trouble to inquire. The thing, however, that struck people most about the rooms was the collection of books—there were books in hundreds, in every available place—on the shelves and in the cupboards, on the tables, on the chairs, and even on the floor. There surely never was such a man for books as my father, and I can see him now, standing before a shelf in the half light of the big dining-room with a volume in his hand, studying it as if he were too much entranced to put it down. He was a tall, thin man, with a pale, thoughtful face, a high forehead, deep-set, curious eyes, that seemed to look you through and through, a big, hooked nose (mine is just like it), a handsome mouth, white teeth, and a heavy, determined-looking chin. He was invariably clean-shaven, well dressed, and so scrupulously neat and natty in his appearance that it seemed hard to imagine he had ever done a stroke of rough work in his life. And yet he could, and did, work harder than most men, but always in the same unostentatious fashion; never saying a word more than was absolutely necessary, but always ready at a moment's notice to pick a quarrel with you, or to say just the very one thing of all others that would be most calculated to give you pain. He was a strange man, was my father.

Of my mother my recollections are less distinct, which is accounted for by the fact that she died when I was only five years old. Indeed, the only remembrance I have of her at all is of a fragile little woman with a pale, sweet face, bending down to kiss me when I was in bed at night.

Drink and temper were my father's chief failings, but I was nearly eight years old before I really found that out. Even to-day, when I shut my eyes, I can conjure up a picture of him sitting in the dining-room before the table, two large candelabras lighting the room, drinking and reciting to himself, not only in English, but in other outlandish tongues that I can only suppose now must have been Latin and Greek. So he would go on until he staggered to his bed, and yet next morning he would be up and about again before sunrise, a little more taciturn, perhaps, and readier to take offence, but otherwise much the same as ever.

That he had always a rooted dislike to me, I know, and I am equally aware that I detested and feared him more than any other living being. For this reason we seldom met. He took his meals in solitary grandeur in the dark, old dining-room, hung round with the dingy pictures that had come out from England, of men in wigs, knickerbockers and queer, long-tailed coats, while I took mine with the old housekeeper in the kitchen lead-ing off the back verandah. We were a strange household, and before I had turned eight years old—as strong an urchin as ever walked—I had come to the conclusion that we were not too much liked or trusted by the folk in the township. My father thought them beneath him, and let them see that he did; they called him proud, and hinted that he was even worse than that. Whether he had anything to be proud of is another matter, and one that I cannot decide. You must judge from the following illustration.

It was early in the year before the great flood which did so much damage in those parts, and which is remembered to this day, that news got about that in a few weeks' time the Governor of the colony would be travelling in our district, and would probably pay our township a visit. A committee of the principal folk was immediately chosen to receive him, and big preparations were made to do him honour. As, perhaps, the chief personage in our little community, my father was asked to preside over their deliberations, and for this purpose a deputation waited upon him. They could not possibly, however, have chosen a more unpropitious moment for their call; my father had been drinking all day, and, when they arrived, he burst into one of his fits of anger and drove them from the house, vowing that he would have nothing at all to do with the affair, and that he would show His Excellency the door if he dared to set foot within his grounds. This act of open hostility produced, as may be supposed, a most unfavourable impression, and my father must have seen it, for he even went so far as to write a note of apology to the committee, and to suggest, as his contribution to the general arrangements, that he should take His Excellency in for the night. Considering the kind of hotels our township boasted in those days, this was no mean offer, and, as may be supposed, it was unhesitatingly accepted.

In due course the Governor arrived with his party. He was received by the committee in the main street under an archway of flags, and, after inspecting the township, rode up the hill with the principal folk towards our house. When he came into the grounds my father went out into the verandah to receive him, and I followed close in his wake, my eyes, I make no doubt, bulging with curiosity. The Governor got off his horse, and at the same moment my father went down the steps. He held out his hand, His Excellency took it, and as he did so looked at him in a very quick and surprised way, just for all the world as if my father were somebody he had seen before, in a very different place, and had never expected to meet again.

'Good gracious, can it be?' he said to himself under his breath, but all the same quite loud enough for me to hear, for I was close beside him. 'Surely you are—'

'My name is Heggarstone,' said my father quickly, an unwonted colour coming into his face, 'and you are His Excellency, the Governor of the colony. If you will allow me, I will make you welcome to my poor abode.'

They looked at each other for a moment, pretty straight, and then the Governor pulled himself together and went into the house, side by side with my father, without another word. Later on, when the dinner given in honour of Her Majesty's representative was over, and the townsfolk had departed, His Excellency and my father sat talking, talking, talking, till far into the night. I could hear the hum of their voices quite distinctly, for my bedroom was next to the dining-room, though, of course, I could not catch what they said.

Next morning, when his horse was at the door, and the escort was standing ready to be off, His Excellency drew my father a little on one side and said in a low voice, so that the others should not hear,—

'And your decision is really final? You will never go back to England to take up your proper position in society?'

'Never!' my father replied, viciously crumpling a handful of creeper leaves as he spoke. 'I have thought it over carefully, and have come to the conclusion that it will be a good thing for society if the name dies out with me. Good-bye.'

'Good-bye,' answered His Excellency, 'and God help you!'

Then he mounted his horse and rode away.

I have narrated this little episode in order to show that I had some justification for believing that my father was not merely the humble, commonplace individual he professed to be. I will now tell you another, which if it did not relieve my curiosity, was surely calculated to confirm my suspicions.

It happened that one day, early in winter, I was in the township at the time when the coach, which now connected us with civilisation, made its appearance. This great event happened twice weekly, and though they had now been familiar with it for some considerable time, the inhabitants, men, women and children, seemed to consider it a point of honour that they should be present, standing in the roadway about the Bushmen's Rest, to receive and welcome it. For my own part I was ten years old, as curious as my neighbours, and above all a highly imaginative child to whom the coach was a thing full of mystery. Times out of number I had pictured myself the driver of it, and often at night, when I was tucked up in my little bed and ought to have been asleep, I could seem to see it making its way through the dark bush, swaying to and fro, the horses stretched out to their full extent in their frenzied gallop.

On this particular occasion there were more passengers than usual, for the reason that a new goldfield had sprung into existence in the ranges to the westward of us, and strangers were passing through our township every day *en route* to it. It was not until the driver had descended from his box and had entered the hotel that the crowd saw fit to disperse. I was about to follow them when I saw, coming towards me, a tall, dignified-looking man whom I had noticed sitting next to the driver when the coach arrived. He boasted a short, close-cropped beard, wore a pair of dark spectacles, and was dressed better than any man I had ever seen in my life before, my father not excepted. In his hand he carried a small portmanteau, and for a moment I thought he was going to enter the Bushmen's Rest like the remainder of the passengers. He changed his mind, however, and after looking about him came towards where I stood.

'My lad,' said he, 'can you tell me which path I should follow to reach Mr Heggarstone's residence?'

My surprise at this question may be better imagined than described. It did not prevent me, however, from answering him.

'My name is Heggarstone,' I said, 'and our house is on the hill over there. You can just see the roof.'

If I had been surprised at his inquiry, it was plain that he was ever so much more astonished when he heard my name. For upwards of half a minute he stood and stared at me as if he did not know what to make of it.

'In that case, if you will permit me,' he said, with curious politeness, 'I will accompany you on your homeward journey. I have come a very long way to see your father, and my business with him is of the utmost importance.'

My first shyness having by this time completely vanished, I gazed at him with undisguised interest. I had not met many travellers in my life, and for this reason when I did I was prepared to make the most of them.

'Have you come from Brisbane, sir?' I inquired, after a short silence, feeling that it was incumbent upon me to say something.

'Just lately,' he answered. 'But before that from London.'

After this magnificent admission, I felt there was nothing more to be said. A man who had come from London to our little township, for the sole purpose of seeing my father, was not the sort of person to be talked to familiarly. I accordingly trudged alongside him in silence, thinking of all the wonderful things he must have seen, and wondering if it would be possible for me at some future date to induce him to tell me about them. At first he must have inclined to the belief that I was rather a forward youth. Now, however, I was as silent as if I were struck dumb. We descended the path to the river without a word, crossed the ford with our tongues still tied, and had almost reached our own boundary fence before either of us spoke. Then my companion moved his bag to the other hand and, placing his right upon my shoulder, said slowly,—

'So you are—well, Marmaduke Heggarstone's son?'

I looked up at him and noticed the gravity of his face as I answered, 'Yes, sir!'

He appeared to ruminate for a few seconds, and my sharp ears caught the words, 'Dear me, dear me!' muttered below his breath. A few moments later we had reached the house, and after I had asked the new-comer to take a seat in the verandah, I went in to find my father and to tell him that a visitor had arrived to see him.

'Who is it?' he inquired, looking up from his book. 'How often am I to tell you to ask people's names before you tell them I am at home? Go back and find out.'

I returned to the verandah, and asked the stranger if he would be kind enough to tell me his name.

'Redgarth,' he said, 'Michael Redgarth. Tell your father that, and I think he will remember me.'

I returned to the dining-room and acquainted my father with what I had discovered. Prepared as I was for it to have some effect upon him, I had no idea the shock would be so great. My father sprang to his feet with what sounded almost like a cry of alarm.

'Redgarth here,' he said; 'what on earth can it mean? However, I'll soon find out.'

So saying he pushed me on one side and went quickly down the passage in the direction of the verandah. My curiosity by this time was thoroughly excited, and I followed him at a respectful distance, frightened lest he should see me and order me back, but resolved that, happen what might, I would discover his mysterious errand.

I saw my father pass through the door out on to the verandah, and as he did so I heard the stranger rise from his chair. What he said by way of introduction I could not catch, but whatever it may have been there could be no doubt that it incensed my father beyond all measure.

'Call me that at your peril,' I heard him say. 'Now tell me your errand here as quickly as you can and be gone again.'

As I stood, listening, in the shadow of the doorway, I could not help thinking that this was rather scurvy treatment on my father's part of one who had come so many thousand miles to see him. However, Mr Redgarth did not seem as much put out by it as I expected he would be.

'I have come to tell you, my—' he began, and then checked himself, 'well, since you wish it, I will call you Mr Heggarstone, that your father is dead.'

'You might have spared yourself the trouble,' my father replied, with a bitter little laugh. 'I knew it a week ago. If that is all you have to tell me I'm sorry you put yourself to so much inconvenience. I suppose my brother sent you?'

'Exactly,' Redgarth replied dryly, 'and a nice business it has been. I traced you to Sydney, and then on to Brisbane. There I had some difficulty in obtaining your address, but as soon as I did so I took the coach and came out here.'

'Well, and now that you have found me what do you want with me?'

'In the first place I am entitled by your brother to say that provided you—'

Here my father must have made some sign to him to stop.

'Pardon my interrupting you,' he said, 'but before we proceed any further let me tell you once and for all that I will have none of my brother's provisoes. Whatever threats, stipulations, or offers he may have empowered you to make, I will have nothing whatsoever to do with them. I washed my hands of my family, as you know, many years ago, and if you had not come now to remind me of the unpleasant fact, I should have allowed myself to forget even that they existed. You know my opinion of my brother. I have had time to think it over, and I see no reason at all for changing it. When we were both younger he ruined my career for me, perjured himself to steal my good name, and as if that were not enough induced my father to back him up in his treatment of me. Go back to them and tell them that I still hate and despise them. Of the name they cannot deprive me, that is one consolation; of the money I will not touch a sixpence. They may have it, every halfpenny, and I wish them joy of it.'

'But have you thought of your son, the little fellow I saw in the township, and who conducted me hither?'

'I have thought of him,' replied my father, sternly, 'and it makes no difference to my decision. I desire him to be brought up in ignorance of his birth. I am convinced that it would be the kinder course. Now I'll wish you a very good evening. If you have any papers with you that you are desirous I should sign, you may send them over to me and I will peruse them with as little delay as possible. I need not warn you to be careful of what you say in the township yonder. They know, and have always known me, as Marmaduke Heggarstone here, and I have no desire that they should become aware of my real name.'

'You need not fear. I shall not tell them,' said Redgarth. 'As for the papers, I have them in this bag. I will leave them with you. You can send them across to me when you have done with them. I suppose it is no use my attempting to make you see the matter in any other light?'

'None whatever.'

'In that case, I have the honour to wish your lor—I mean to wish you, Mr Heggarstone, a very good evening.'

As he spoke I heard him buckle the straps of his portmanteau, and then I slipped noiselessly down the passage towards the kitchen. A moment later his step sounded upon the gravel and he was gone.

On the Thursday following he left the township, and we saw no more of him. Whatever his errand may have been, never once during his lifetime did my father say anything to me upon the subject, nor did I ever venture to question him about it. Perhaps, as he said, there is something behind it all that I am happier in not knowing. So far as I have ever heard such skeletons are generally best left in un-disturbed possession of their cupboards.

After that we resumed the same sort of life as had been our portion before his arrival.

This monotonous existence continued un-disturbed until the time of the great flood, which, as I have said before, is even re-membered to this day. It occurred at the end of a wet season, and after a fortnight's pouring rain, which continued day and night. Never was such rain known, and for this reason the ground soon became so thoroughly saturated that it could absorb no more. In consequence the creeks filled, and all the billabongs became deep as lakes.

In order to realise what follows you must understand that above the township, perhaps a couple of miles or so, three creeks joined forces, and by so doing formed the Cargoo River, on the banks of which our township was located. There had been heavy rain on all these creeks, and in consequence they came down bankers, united, as I have just said, and then, being penned in by the hills and backed up by the stored water in the billabongs, swept down the valley towards the township in one great flood, which carried everything before it.   Never shall I forget that night.   The clouds had cleared off the sky earlier in the evening, and it was as bright as day, the moon being almost at the full. I was having my supper with old Betty in the kitchen when suddenly I heard an odd sort of rumbling in the distance.   I stopped eating to listen.   Even to my childish ears the sound was peculiar, and as it still continued, I asked Betty, who was my oracle in everything, what she thought it meant.   She was a little deaf, and suggested the wind in the trees. But I knew that this was no wind in trees. Every moment it was growing louder, and when I left the kitchen and went through the house to the front verandah, where I found my father standing looking up the valley, it had grown into a well-defined roar.   I questioned him on the subject.

'It is a flood,' he answered, half to himself. 'Nothing but water, and an enormous body of it, could make that sound.'

The words were scarcely out of his mouth before a man on horseback appeared round the bend of the hill and galloped up the path.   His horse was white with foam, and as he drew up before the steps he shouted wildly,—

'The flood is coming down the valley. Fly for your lives.'

My father only laughed—a little scornfully, I thought—and said, in his odd, mocking voice,—

'No flood will touch us here, my friend, but if you are anxious to do humanity a service, you had better hasten on and warn the folk in the township below us. They are in real danger!'

Long before he had finished speaking, the man had turned his horse and was galloping down the track, as fast as he had come, towards the little cluster of houses we could discern in the hollow below us. That young man was Dennis O'Rourke, the eldest son of a Selector further up the valley, and the poor fellow was found, ten days later, dead, entangled in the branches of a gum tree, twenty miles below Barranda Township, with a stirrup iron bent round his left foot, and scarcely half a mile from his own selection gate. Without doubt he had been overtaken by the flood before he could reach his wife to give her the alarm. In consequence, the water caught her unprepared, she was never seen again, and only one of her children escaped alive ; their homestead, which stood on the banks of the creek, was washed clean off the face of the earth, and when I rode down that way on my pony, after the flood had subsided, it would have been impossible to distinguish the place where it had once stood.

But to return to my narrative. O'Rourke had not left us five minutes before the rumbling had increased to a roar, almost like that of thunder. And every second it was growing louder. Then, with a suddenness no man could imagine who has never seen such a thing, a solid wall of water, shining like silver in the moonlight, came into view, seemed to pause for a moment, and then swept trees, houses, cattle, haystacks, fences, and even large boulders before it like so much driftwood. Within a minute of making its appearance it had spread out across the valley, and, most marvellous part of all, had risen half way up the hill, and was throwing a line of yeast-like foam upon our garden path. A few seconds later we distinctly heard it catch the devoted township, and the crashing and rending sound it made was awful to hear. Then the noise ceased, and only a swollen sheet of angry water, stretching away across the valley for nearly a mile and a half was to be seen. Such a flood no man in the district, and I state this authoritatively, had ever in his life experienced before. Certainly I have not seen one like it since. And the brilliant moonlight only intensified the terrible effect.

Having assured himself that we had nothing to fear, my father ordered me off to bed, and reluctantly I went—only to lie curled up in my warm blankets thinking of the waters outside, and repicturing the effect produced upon my mind by O'Rourke's sensational arrival. It was the first time I had ever seen a man under the influence of a life-and-death excitement, and, imaginative child as I was, the effect it produced on my mind was not one to be easily shaken off. Then I must have fallen asleep, for I have no recollection of anything else till I was awakened in the middle of the night by the noise of people entering my room. Half-asleep and half-awake I sat up, rubbing my eyes, and blinking at the brightness of the candle my father carried in his hand. Old Betty was with him, and behind them, carrying a bundle in his arms, stalked a tall, thin man with a grey beard, long hair and a white, solemn face. His clothes, I noticed, were sopping wet, and a stream of water marked his progress across the floor.

'Take James out and put the child in his

place,' said my father, coming towards my bed. The man advanced, and Betty lifted me out and placed me on a chair. The bundle was then tucked up where I had been, and, when that had been done, Betty turned to me.

'Jim,' she said, 'you must be a good boy and give no trouble, and I'll make you up a nice bed in the corner.' This was accordingly done, and when it was ready I was put into it, and in five minutes had forgotten the interruption and was fast asleep once more.

As usual, directly there was light in the sky, I woke and looked about me. To my surprise, however, for I had for the moment forgotten the strange waking of the night, I found myself, not in my own place, but on a pile of rugs in the corner. Wondering what this might mean, I looked across at my bed, half-expecting to find it gone. But no! There it stood, sure enough, with an occupant I could not remember ever to have seen before—a little rose-leaf of a girl, at most not more than four years old. Like myself she was sitting up, staring with her great blue eyes, and laughing from under a tangled wealth of golden curls at my astonishment. Her little pink and white face, so charmingly dimpled, seemed prettier than anything I had ever seen or dreamed of before; but I did not know what to make of it all, and, boy-like, was inordinately shy. Seeing this, and not being accustomed to be slighted, the little minx climbed out of bed, and, with her tiny feet peeping from beneath one of my flannel night-shirts, came running across to where I lay. Then standing before me, her hands behind her back, she said in a baby voice—that I can hear now even after twenty years,—

'I'se Sheilah!'

And that was my introduction to the good angel of my life. Five minutes later we were playing together on the floor as if we had been friends for years instead of minutes. And when Betty came into the room, according to custom, to carry me off to my bath, her first remark was one which has haunted me all my life, and will go on doing so until I die.

'Pretty dears,' she cried, 'sure they're just made for each other.'

And so we were!

It was not until some time later that I learnt how it was that old McLeod and his baby daughter came to be under our roof that night. This was the reason of it. The man and his wife, it appears, were but new arrivals in the colony, and were coming out our way to settle.

They were finishing their last day's stage down the valley when the flood caught the bullock dray, drowned his wife and all the cattle, and well-nigh finished the father and child, who were carried for miles clinging to a tree, to be eventually washed up before our house. My father, standing in the verandah, heard a cry for help, and waded out into the water just in time to save them. Having done this he brought them up to the house, and, as there was nowhere else to put her, I was turned out and Sheilah was given my bed.

Next morning a foaming sea of water cut us off from the township, or what few houses remained of it, and for this reason it was manifestly impossible that old McLeod could continue his journey. I remember that poor, little motherless Sheilah and I played together all day long in the verandah, as happy as two birds, while her father watched us from a deep chair, with grave, tear-stained eyes. In the death of his wife he had sustained a grievous loss, from which somehow I don't think he ever thoroughly recovered.

Three days later the water fell as rapidly as it had risen, and as soon as it had suffi-ciently abated, McLeod, having thanked my father for his hospitality, which I could not help thinking had been grudgingly enough bestowed, took Sheilah in his arms, right up from the middle of our play, and tramped off, a forlorn black figure, down the path towards the township. As far as the turn of the track, and until the scrub timber hid her from my gaze, I could see the little mite waving her hand to me in farewell.

That week McLeod purchased Gregory's farm on the other side of the township, and installed himself in the house on the knoll overlooking the river, taking care this time to choose a position that was safely out of water reach. Once he had settled in, I was as often to be found there as at my own home, and continued to be Sheilah's constant companion and playmate from that time forward.

And so the years went by, every one finding us firmer friends. It was I who held her while she took her first ride upon the old grey pony McLeod bought for the boy to run up the milkers on. It was I who taught her to row the cranky old tub they called a boat on the Long Reach; it was I who baited the hook that caught her first fish; it was I who taught her the difference in the nests in the trees behind the homestead, and how to distinguish between the birds that built them; in everything I was her guide, philosopher and her constant friend. And surely there never was so sweet a child to teach as Sheilah—her quickness was extraordinary, and, bush-bred boy though I was, it was not long before she was my equal at everything where strength was not absolutely required. By the time she was twelve and I sixteen, she could have beaten any other girl in the township at anything they pleased, and, what made them the more jealous, her beauty was becoming more and more developed every day. Even in the hottest sun her sweet complexion seemed to take no hurt, and now the hair, that I remembered curling closely round her head on the morning when we first became acquainted, descended like a fall of rippling gold far below her shoulders. And her eyes—but there, surely there never were such eyes as Sheilah's—for truth and innocence. Oh, Sheilah, my own sweetheart, if only we could have foreseen then all the bitterness and agony of the rocky path that we were some day to tread, what would we not have done to ward off the fatal time? But, of course, we could not see it, and so we went on blindfold upon our happy-go-lucky way, living only in the present, and having no thought of the cares of the morrow. And the strangest part about it all was that, thrown together continually as we were, neither of us had taken any account of love. The little god had so far kept his arrows in his quiver. But he was to shoot them soon enough in all conscience.

To say that my father forbade my intercourse with the McLeods would not be the truth. But if I said that he lost no opportunity of sneering at the old man and his religion (he was a Dissenter of the most vigorous description, and used to preach on Sundays in the township) I should not be overstepping the mark.

I don't believe there was another man in the world who could sneer as could my father. He had cultivated that accomplishment to perfection, and in a dozen words would bring me to such a pitch of indignation that it was as much as I could do to refrain from laying violent hands upon him. I can see him now lying back in his chair in the old dining-room, when he was hearing me my lessons (for he taught me all I know), a book half-closed upon his knee, looking me up and down with an expression upon his face that seemed to say, 'Who ever would have thought I should have been plagued with such a dolt of a son!' Then, as likely as not, he would lose his temper over my stupidity, box my ears, and send me howling from the room, hating him with all the intensity of which my nature was capable. I wonder if ever a boy before had so strange and unnatural a parent.

CHAPTER II

HOW I FIRST LEARNED MY LOVE FOR SHEILAH

It was the morning of my eighteenth birthday, and, to celebrate it, Sheilah and I had long before made up our minds to ride to, and spend the day at, the Blackfellow's Cave—a large natural cavern in the mountains, some fifteen or sixteen miles distant from the township. It was one of our favourite jaunts, and according to custom we arranged to start early.

For this reason, as soon as light was in the sky, I was astir, took a plunge in the creek, and then ran down to the paddock and caught the horse I intended riding that day—a fine, well set-up thoroughbred of our own breeding. And, by the same token, there were no horses like ours in the district, either for looks, pace, stamina, or pedigree. What my father did not know about horse and cattle breeding no man in the length and breadth of Australia could teach him. And a good bushman he was too, for all his scholarly ways and habits, a first-class rider, and second to none in his work among the beasts in the stockyard. All I know myself I learnt from him, and I should be less than grateful if I were above owning it. But that has nothing to do with my story. Having caught my horse, I took him up to the stable and put a first-class polish on him with the brush, then, fastening him up to the bough-shade to be ready when I wanted him, hurried in to my breakfast. When I entered the room my father was already seated at the table. He received me after his usual fashion, which was to look me up and down, smile in a way that was quite his own, and then, with a heavy sigh, return to his reading as if it were a matter of pain to him to have any-thing at all to do with me. When we were half through the meal he glanced up from his book, and said,—

'As soon as you've done your breakfast, you'd better be off and muster Kidgeree paddock. If you come across Bates's bull bring him in with you and let him remain in the yard until I see him.'

This was not at all what I had looked for-ward to on my birthday, so I said,—

'I can't muster to-day. It's my birthday, and I'm going out.'

He stared at me for nearly a minute without speaking, and then said with a sneer,—

'I'm sure I very much regret that I should have inadvertently interfered with your arrangements. Miss McLeod accompanies you, of course!'

'I am going out with Sheilah! Yes!'

Again he was silent for a few moments—then he looked up once more.

'As it is your birthday of course you consider you have an excuse for laziness. Well, I suppose you must go, but if you should chance to honour the father with your society you might point out to him that, on two occasions this week, his sheep have been on my frontage.'

'It's our own fault; we should mend our boundary.'

'Indeed! And pray how long have you been clear-headed enough to see that?'

'Anyone could see it. It's not fair to blame Mr McLeod for what is not his fault.'

'Dear me! This perspicuity is really most pleasing. An unexpected Daniel come to judgment, I declare. Well, at anyrate, I'll give you a note to take to the snuffling old hound and in it I'll tell him that the next beast of his I catch on my property I'll shoot. That's a fair warning. You can come in for it when you are starting.'

'I shall not take it.'

'Indeed! I am sorry to hear that. Your civility is evidently on a par with your industry.'

Then, seeing that I had risen, he bowed ironically, and wished me a 'very good morning.'

I did not answer, but marched out of the room, my cheeks flushed with passion. Nothing, I knew, gave him greater pleasure than to let him see that he had hurt me, and yet, do what I would, I could not prevent myself from showing it.

Having passed through the house, I went into the kitchen to obtain from Betty, who still constituted the female element of our household, some provender for the day. This obtained, I saddled my horse, strapped a quart pot on to my saddle, mounted, and rode off. As I passed the front of the house I heard my father call to me to stop, but I did not heed him, and rode on down the track to the ford, thence, through the township, to McLeod's selection.

And now a few words about the latter's

homestead—the house which has played such a prominent part in my life's drama. I think I have already told you that it stood on the top of a small rise about a quarter of a mile above the river and looked right up the valley over the township roofs, just in the opposite direction to ours. In the twelve years that McLeod had lived there he had added considerably to it—a room here and there—till it had grown into a rambling, disconnected, but charming, old place, overgrown with creepers, and nestling in a perfect jungle of peppermint trees, gums, oranges and bamboos. The stockyard, for the selection carried about five hundred cattle and a couple of thousand sheep, was located at the back, with the stables and Sheilah's poultry-yard; and it had always been one of my greatest pleasures to be allowed to go down and give the old man a hand with his mustering or branding; to help Sheilah run up the milkers, or to hunt for eggs in the scrub with her when the hens escaped and laid outside.

Reaching the slip panels I jumped off and tied my horse to the fence; then went up the shady path towards the house. Bless me! how the memory of that morning comes back as I sit talking now. The hot sun, for it was the middle of summer, was streaming through the foliage and dancing on the path; there was the creeper-covered verandah, with its chairs and old-fashioned sofa inviting one to make oneself at home, and, last but not least, there was Sheilah standing waiting for me, dressed in her dark green habit and wearing a big straw hat upon her pretty head.

'You're late, Jim,' she said, for, however much she might spoil me, Sheilah always made a point of telling me my faults, 'I've been waiting for you nearly half-an-hour.'

'I'm sorry, Sheilah,' I answered. 'I could not get away as soon as I expected.'

I did not tell her what had really made me so late; for somehow, even if I did think badly of my father myself, I had no wish that other people should do so too.

'But I am forgetting,' she continued, 'I ought first to have wished you many happy returns of the day, dear old Jim, and have scolded you afterwards.'

'Somehow I never seem to take offence however much you scold, Sheilah,' I said, as we left the verandah and went round by the neat path to the stables.

'Then it's not much use my trying to do you any good, is it?' she answered with a little laugh.

We found her pretty bay pony standing

waiting at the rails, and when she was ready I swung her up into the saddle like a bird. Then mounting my own horse, off we went down the track, through the wattle scrub, across the little bubbling creek that joined the big river a bit below the township, and finally away through the Mulga towards the mountains and the Blackfellow's Cave.

It was a breathless morning—the beginning of a typical Australian summer day. In the trees overhead the cicadas chirped, parroquets and wood pigeons flew swiftly across our path; now and again we almost rode over a big silly kangaroo, who went blundering away at what looked a slow enough pace, but was in reality one that would have made a good horse do all he knew to keep up with him. Our animals were in splendid trim and, in spite of the heat, we swung easily along, side by side, laughing and chattering, as if we had never known a care in our lives. Indeed, I don't know that we had then. At least not as I understand cares now.

About ten o'clock we halted for half-an-hour in the shadow of a big gum, and alongside a pretty water-hole. Then, continuing our ride, we reached the Blackfellow's Cave about mid-day.

How the cave received its name must remain a mystery; personally, I never remember to have seen a black fellow within half-a-dozen miles of it. In fact, I believe they invariably avoided it, being afraid of meeting 'debil-debils' in its dark and gloomy interior.

On arrival, we hobbled our horses out, lit a fire, and, as soon as we had procured water from a pool hard by, set our quart pot on to boil. This done, we made tea, ate our lunch, and then marched in to explore the cavern. It was a queer enough place in all conscience, cave leading from cave and passage from passage, and for each we had our own particular name—the church, the drawing-room, the coach-house, and a dozen others. Some were pitch dark, and necessitated our lighting the candle Sheilah had brought with her, others were open at the top, enabling us, through the aperture, to see the bright blue sky overhead. From one to another we wandered, trying the echoes, and making each resound with the noises of our voices. The effects produced were most weird, and I could not help thinking that any black fellow who might have penetrated inside would soon have collected material for 'debil-debil' yarns sufficient to last him and his tribe for generations.

At last, having thoroughly explored everything we made our way out into the open air once more. By this time it was nearly three o'clock and a terribly hot afternoon. Not a a breath of wind stirred the leaves, while the parched earth seemed to throw back the sun's scorching rays with all the fierceness of a burning-glass. It was too hot even for the birds, and though we could hear the monotonous cawing of crows in the distance, and the occasional chatter of the parakeets, not one was visible; indeed, when an old-man kangaroo hopped on to the little plateau before the cave's mouth, and saw us, it was nearly half-a-minute before he could find sufficient energy to hop away again. The cicadas were still busy in the trees, and in the dead atmosphere their chirrup seemed to echo half across the world.

When it was time for us to think of returning home, we crossed to where our horses were standing idly whisking their tails under a big gum, and having saddled them, mounted and started on our journey. We had not, however, proceeded more than five miles before thick clouds rose in the sky, driven by a strong wind that rustled the dry twigs and grass, and sent the dust flying about our ears like so much small shot.

Suddenly Sheilah brought her pony to a standstill and began to sniff the wind.

'What is it?' I asked, stopping my horse and looking round at her. 'What do you smell?'

'Burning grass,' she answered. And as she spoke I got a distinct whiff of it myself.

'There's a fire somewhere,' she said; 'I hope it's not coming our way.'

'It is probably on the top of the ranges,' I answered. 'And the wind's funnelling it down to us.'

For some time we rode on in silence, the smell growing stronger and stronger as we progressed. Overhead, dense smoke was floating towards us, while the air was becoming momentarily hotter.

'It is a fire, and a big one,' I said, pulling my horse up again and signing to Sheilah to do the same. 'The question is whether we are wise in going on, without first finding out which way it is coming.'

'It's somewhere in the gully ahead of us,' said Sheilah. 'Let us proceed as far as we can.'

Accordingly we rode on, the smoke getting every moment thicker, and the heat more powerful. Presently we reached a slight eminence, from which we knew we should be able to command a good view of the gully we were about to enter. As we ascended the little rise, however, something caught my eye, and I turned and shouted to Sheilah—

'Round—round, and ride for your life!'

As I spoke I wheeled my horse and she followed my example—but not before we had both seen a thin line of fire run through the dry grass not fifty yards from where we stood. Next moment there was an awful blaze behind us, and our terrified horses were dashing down the gully, as fast as they could lay their legs to the ground. It was perilous going, over rocks and logs, across rain chasms and between trees, but heedless of anything we rode on at breakneck speed, knowing that we were racing for our very lives. And the flames came after us with the fury and noise of an express train. When we had gone about a hundred yards I looked at Sheilah. She was sitting back in her saddle, her mouth firmly set, steering her terrified and almost unmanageable pony with all the skill and dexterity of which she was mistress.

As we turned the corner I looked back and saw that the fire had stretched high up the hills on either side, while it was also sweeping down the valley behind us with terrifying rapidity. Fast as we were going, the flames were overtaking us. What were we to do to escape? The heat was so intense that it was sapping every atom of strength out of the horses, and one crash into a tree, one stumble in a hole, one little mistake and the result would be an awful and agonising death. On all sides were terrified animals—cattle, horses, sheep, kangaroo, emu, wallabies, dingoes even, all like ourselves flying for their lives, while overhead thousands of birds flew screeching before the hot blast. I endeavoured to keep my horse by the side of Sheilah's in order to be ready to help her in case of accident, but it was almost an impossibility. Seeing that we might be separated I called to her.

'Steer to your left, and if possible try to reach the cave.'

She nodded to let me see that she understood, and then on we went as before. Strong man as I was, the heat behind, the choking smoke and the awful glare all round were almost more than I could bear, and I dared not think of their effect on Sheilah. But whatever her sufferings may have been, she was riding as carefully as if nothing out of the common were occurring.

Leaving a little bit of open ground we plunged into the scrub again, but had not gone twenty paces in it before an awful thing happened. Sheilah's pony, who for the last hundred yards had been going very heavily, now put his foot into a hole and went down with a crash, throwing the girl over his head a dozen feet or more. With a cry of terror I pulled my horse to a standstill, and jumped off, but Sheilah lay as if she were dead, her legs curled up under her and her head curiously twisted round. The pony was screaming with agony where he had fallen. What was to be done? There was not an instant to be lost. Dragging my own frightened horse over to where she lay, I picked her up. She was unconscious and for a moment I thought the fall had broken her neck. Then I turned to her poor pony, who by this time had struggled to his feet. One glance told me the worst. He had broken his off fore leg and it was useless counting further on him for assistance. Here was a terrible position. As far as I could see only one thing was to be done. The flames were drawing closer and closer— there was scarcely time for thought. A large log lay near at hand. I backed my horse against it, and then lifting poor Sheilah in my arms, placed her on his wither and climbed into the saddle. Being only a youngster and very high-spirited, he did not take very kindly to this curious proceeding, but I forced him to it with a strength and determination I did not know that I possessed, and then, holding Sheilah in my arms, off we went again, leaving her own pony to meet his fate from the on-rushing flames.

If my ride had been difficult before, I will leave you to imagine how much more peril-ous it was now that I had not only to guide my horse in order to escape low hanging branches and other dangers, but at the same time to hold Sheilah in her place. She lay with her pretty head hanging over my arm, as white and still as death.

On—on we dashed for our very lives. The pace had been fast before—now, even with the additional burden my animal had to bear, it was terrific. But I knew we could not be more than a couple of miles at furthest from the cave. If he only could keep it up till then, it was just possible we might be saved.

But even as this thought passed through my brain I felt his powers begin to fail. The old elasticity was quite gone, and I had to rouse him with my voice and heel. Oh,

how awful seemed my utter helplessness—
my life, Sheilah's life, her father's happiness,
all depending on the strength, pluck and
endurance of an uncomprehending animal.
I called him by name; in an ecstasy of fear
I even promised him perpetual ease for the
rest of his equine existence if only he would
carry me as far as the cave.   And then it
was, in that moment of despair, when death
seemed inevitable for both of us, that I discovered that I loved Sheilah with something
more than the brotherly affection I had always
supposed myself to entertain for her.   Yes!
I was a man and she was a woman, and with
all the certainty of a man's knowledge, I
knew that I loved her then.   On, on brave
horse and give that love a chance of ripen-
ing.   On, on, though the clammy sweat of
death bedews and paralyses thy nostrils, on,
on, for on thy courage and endurance de-
pends the happiness of two human lives.

By this time the wind had risen to the
strength of a hurricane and this could
only mean that the flames would travel
proportionately faster.   They could not be
more than half a mile behind us now at the
greatest calculation, and the cave was, perhaps,
half that distance ahead.   It was a race for

life with the odds against us, but at all hazards, even if I had to lay down my own to do it, I knew that Sheilah must be saved. Looking back on it now I can truthfully say that that was my one and only thought. On and on we went—the horse lurching in his stride, his powers failing him with every step; and yet we dared not dismount, for I knew that I could not run fast enough with Sheilah in my arms to stand any possible chance of saving her.

At last we turned the corner of the gully, and could see before us, scarcely more than a hundred yards distant, the black entrance to the cave. I looked round, and as I did so saw a narrow tongue of fire lick out and seize upon the grass scarcely fifty yards behind us. Great beads of sweat rose upon my forehead; blisters, caused by the intense heat, were forming on my neck; my hat was gone, and my horse's strength was failing him with every stride. God help us, for we were in desperate straits. And only a hundred yards lay between us and safety. Then I felt the animal under me pause, and give a shiver—he struggled on for a few yards, and then down in a heap he went without more ado, throwing us gently from him in his fall.

Death was surely only a matter of a few moments now. However, I was not going to die without a struggle.

Springing up I again took Sheilah in my arms, and set off with her as fast as I could run towards the cave. Short distance though it was, it seemed an eternity before I had toiled to the top of the little hill, crossed the plateau, and was laying my precious burden upon the ground inside the cave. Then I fell beside her, too much exhausted to care very much what became of me. As I did so, I heard the fire catch great trees outside, and presently little flames came licking up almost to the entrance of the cave where we lay. Still Sheilah remained unconscious, and for some few moments I was but little better. As soon, however, as my strength returned to me, I picked her up again and bore her through the first cave into the second, where it was comparatively light and cool. Leaving her alone here for a minute I picked my way into the third cave, where there was a small pool of spring water. From this I took a deep draught, and then, wetting my handkerchief thoroughly, hurried back to Sheilah's side. Thereupon I set to work to bathe her hands and face, but for some time without any satisfactory result. Then her eyes opened, and she looked about her. At first she seemed scarcely to comprehend where she was, or what had happened, but her memory soon came back to her, and as she heard the roar of the fire outside and felt the hot blast sweeping into the cave, a great shudder swept over her.

'Ah! I remember now!' she said. 'I had a fall. What has become of poor Rorie?'

'We had to leave him behind.'

She put her little hands up to her eyes, as if to shut out the dreadful picture my words had conjured up.

'But how did you get me here?' she asked.

'I carried you on my saddle before me till my own horse dropped,' I said, 'and then I brought you the rest of the distance in my arms.'

She closed her eyes and was silent for a minute or so, then she opened them again and turned to me with a womanliness I had never before remarked in her.

'Jim,' she said, laying her little hand upon my arm, 'you have saved my life! As long as I live I will never forget what you have done for me to-day!'

From that moment she was no longer

Sheilah, my old playfellow and almost sister. She was Sheilah, the goddess—the one woman to be loved by me for the remainder of my life.

I took her hand and kissed it. Then everything seemed to swim round me—a great darkness descended upon me, and I fell back in a dead faint.

When I recovered myself and was able to move, I left her and went into the outer cave. The fire had passed, and was sweeping on its way down the gully, leaving behind it a waste of blackened earth, and in many cases still flaring timber. But prudence told me that the ground was still far too hot to be safe for walking on. So I went back to Sheilah, and we sat talking about our narrow escape until nightfall.

Then just as we were wondering how, since we had no horses, we could best make our way home, a shout echoed in the outer cave, and we ran there to be confronted by McLeod, my father and half-a-dozen other township men who had come out in search of us. Sheilah flew to her father's arms, while I looked anxiously, I must confess, at mine. But, whether he felt any emotion or not, he allowed no sign to escape him. He only held out his hand, and said dryly,—

'This, you see, is the outcome of your obstinacy.'

Then he turned and called to a black boy, who stood outside holding a horse. The lad brought the animal up, and my father signed to me to mount, which I did, and presently we were all making our way home.

At the entrance to the township, where we were to separate, I stopped the animal I was riding and turned to Sheilah to say good-bye. She drew the horse her father had brought for her up alongside mine, and said softly,—

'Good-bye, and God bless you, Jim! Whatever may happen in the future, I shall never forget what you have done for me to-day.'

Then old McLeod, who had heard from Sheilah all about our ride for life, came up and thanked me in his old-fashioned way for having saved his daughter's life, and after that we rode home, my father and I, silently, side by side. As soon as supper was over, I went to bed, thoroughly worn out, but the stirring events of the day had been too much for me, and so hour after hour I lay tossing about, unable to sleep. At last I dozed off, only to be wakened a short while later by a curious sound coming from my father's room. Not knowing what it might be, I sprang from my bed and went into the verandah, where I had a clear view into his apartment. And a curious sight it was that I saw.

My father was kneeling at his bedside, his head hidden in his hands, praying as if his whole life depended on it. His hands were white with the tenacity of their grip on each other, and his whole figure quivered under the influence of his emotion. When he raised his head I saw that his face was stained with tears and that others were still coursing down his cheeks. But the reason of it all was more than I could tell.

Having satisfied my curiosity, and feeling somehow rather ashamed of myself for having watched him, I went back to bed and fell fast asleep, not to wake next morning till the sun was high in the sky.

CHAPTER III

AFTER the events described in the preceding chapter it was a new life that Sheilah opened up for me—one as different from that which had existed before as could well be imagined. Every moment I could spare from my work (and I was generally pretty busy for the reason that my father was increasing in years and he had resigned a large measure of the management of his property to me) was spent in her company. I thought of her all day and dreamed of her all night.

For two important reasons, however, I was compelled to keep my love a secret, both from herself and from the world in general. My father would have laughed the very notion of an engagement to scorn, and without his consent I was in less than in no position at all to marry. Therefore I said nothing on the subject to anybody.

And now having introduced you to the good angel of my life, I must do the same for the reverse character.

About two years after the bush fire described in the last chapter, there came to our township, whither nobody was ever able to discover, a man who was destined to exercise a truly sinister influence upon my life.

In appearance he presented a strange individuality, being of medium stature, with a queer sort of Portuguese face, out of which two dark eyes glittered like those of a snake. He arrived in the township late one summer evening, mounted on a fine upstanding bay mare and followed by a couple of the most diabolical-looking black boys any man could possibly set eyes on, stayed the night at the grog shanty, and early next morning rode off up the hill as far as Merther's old homestead, which it was said he had taken for a term of years. Whatever its intrinsic advantages may have been, it was a queer place for a man to choose; firstly, because of the strange stories that were told about it, and secondly, because it had stood empty for nearly five years and was reported to be overrun by snakes, rats and scorpions. But Whispering Pete, by which name he afterwards became known to us (from a peculiar habit he had of speaking in a voice but little louder than a whisper) seemed to have no objection to either the rumours or the vermin, but just went his way—doing a bit of horse and cattle dealing as the chances turned up—never interfering with his neighbours, and only showing him self in the township when compelled by the exigencies of his business to do so.

It was not until some considerable time after the events which it is my purpose to describe to you now that I heard the stories, that were told about him, but when I did I could easily credit their truth. Among other peculiarities the man was an ardent and clever musician, and strangely enough, considering his brutality towards grown-up people, a great lover of children. It was well known that the little ones could do more with him in five minutes than anyone else could hope to do in a lifetime. Women, I believe, had never filled any place in his life. The following episode in his career will, I fancy give you a better notion of his character than any amount of explanation upon my part could do.

Somewhere on the Murray River, Pete, who was then running a flash hotel for squatters and skippers of the river steamers, managed to get himself into hot water with the police on a charge of working an illicit still. They had had suspicions of him for some considerable time, but, knowing the character of their man, had waited in order to make certain before effecting his arrest. One of his acquaintances, however, a man, who for some reason or another bore him no good will, put them on the right track, and now all they had to do was to ride up to his residence and take him into custody. By the time they reached it, however, Pete had been warned by somebody and had taken to the bush to be out of the way. He did not return to the neighbourhood but left South Australia forthwith, and migrated into New South Wales, where he embarked upon a new career, much to the relief of the man who had betrayed him, whose life, as you may imagine, had up to this time been cursed with the very real fear of Pete's revenge.

The months went slowly by, Pete was not heard of again, and at last it so happened that this self-same individual was also compelled, by the exigencies of his business, to leave South Australia, and to cross into the oldest Colony, where, being a sanguine man, he hoped to lay the foundation of a fortune. By the time he reached his destination Pete was once more an outlaw, and the police were looking for him, but on what charge I cannot now remember. It is sufficient that he was known to be in hiding near the identical township where his old enemy had taken up his abode. Of course, when the latter made his choice and had fixed upon this particular locality, he did not know this; but he was to learn it before very long, and in a manner that was destined to prove highly unpleasant, if not dangerous, to himself and his family.

It was a terribly hot summer that year, and the country was burnt up to a cinder; bush fires were of almost daily occurrence, and the loss of life during that particular season was, so the oldest inhabitants asserted, exceptional. Beeton, the new-comer—the man who had betrayed Pete in South Australia, as narrated, nearly two years before — had taken up a selection some few miles outside the township, had built himself a homestead, and had settled down in it with his wife and family, blissfully unconscious that the man whom he dreaded meeting more than he would have done the Father of Evil himself was hidden in a large cavern in the ranges scarcely ten miles, as the crow flies, from his own verandah steps. He imagined that everything was safe, and went about his daily work feeling as contented with his lot in life as any man who takes up new country and begins to work it can expect to be. The sword, however, which was suspended above his head by a single hair, was beginning to tremble, and would fall before very long and cut him to pieces in so doing.

Now it had so happened that in the old days in South Australia, when Pete and Beeton had still been friends, the former had been a constant playfellow of the latter's youngest child, a bewitching little girl of two, who returned with interest the affection the other bestowed upon her. Two days before Christmas, this mite, now nearly three years old, strayed away from her home and was lost in the scrub. Search parties were organised and sent out in every direction, but without success; look where they would, they could find no trace of her. And for a very good reason.

All the time they were hunting for her she was safe and sound in Pete's cavern. The outlaw had found her when she was about ten miles from home, and had conveyed her there with all possible speed. He was well aware what he was doing, for the child had recognised him at once, and he had never forgotten her It would probably have surprised some of those who were wont to regard him with so much apprehension could they have seen him during the evening, playing with his little guest upon the floor of the cavern; and later on, seated by her side, telling her fairy stories until she began to feel sleepy, when she insisted upon saying her prayers to him, and compelled him to listen with all the gravity at his command.

The following morning he made up his mind, mounted his horse and, lifting the child up before him, set off through the scrub in the direction of the father's selection. Reaching the boundary fence, from which the house could be easily seen, he kissed the youngster and set her down, bidding her run home as fast as she could go and let her mother see that she was none the worse for her adventure. When he had made sure that she had reached her destination, he wheeled his horse and set off on his return journey to the ranges. As he did so he saw the signs of a bush fire rising above the trees ahead of him, dense clouds of smoke were rolling up into the azure sky, and, as if to make the danger more complete, the wind was freshening every minute. A quarter-of-an-hour later it looked as if his fate were sealed. Behind him was civilisation, with its accompaniment of police; ahead, and on either hand, the fire and seemingly certain destruction by one of the most terrible deaths imaginable. What was he to do? It did not take him very long, however, to make up his mind. At one spot, a couple of miles or so to his left, the smoke was not so heavy, and his knowledge of the country told him the reason of this. It was due to a dry watercourse in which there was nothing that would burn. Urging his horse forward he made for it as fast as he could go. But he was not destined to get there quite as quickly as he expected, for, when he was only a hundred yards or so distant from the bank, his quick eye detected the body of a man lying on the ground beneath a casuarina tree. With his habitual carelessness of human life he was about to leave him to be dealt with by the on-rushing flames, when he chanced to catch sight of the other's face. Then he pulled his horse to a standstill, as if he had been shot. The individual on the ground was Beeton, the man who had betrayed him in South Australia, and the father of the child whom he had risked so much that day to save. The recognition was mutual, for the man, though quite incapable of moving (he had broken his right leg, so it transpired later) was still conscious. Here was a glorious chance of revenge, and one of which Pete was just the sort of man to take the fullest advantage. He brought his terrified horse a little closer, and lolling in his saddle looked calmly down on his prostrate foe.

'How d'ye do, Beeton?' he said, with the easy familiarity of an old acquaintance, to all intents and purposes quite oblivious to the fact that an enormous bush fire was raging in their vicinity, and was every second drawing closer to them. 'It is some time since we last had the pleasure of meeting, or my memory deceives me. Let me see, I think it was in South Australia, was it not?'

Beeton's complexion was even whiter than it had been before as he glanced up at his enemy and marked the relentless look upon his face. He did not answer, however.

'Looks as if you've been inconsiderate enough to have forgotten the circumstance,' continued Pete, mockingly, 'and yet, if I'm not making a mistake, there was every reason why you should have remembered it. However, that does not matter; it seems as if I'm to have a chance of getting even with you after all. D'you see yonder fire? Well it will pass this way in a few minutes. There's only one chance of escape and that is to make your way into the creek bed yonder. I should advise you to hurry up and get there unless you wish to be roasted to a cinder.'

'Curse you, you can see I'm done for and can't move,' cried the other in a tone of agony. 'If you were not the devil you are, you would help me to get there. But you will leave me to die, I know.'

'Why should I help you?' inquired Pete, with continued calmness. 'Who was it put the police on my track at Yackamunda, eh—and drove me out here? Why, you did! And now you want me to save you. No, my lad, you can lie there and burn for all I care or will help you.'

'Then be off,' cried the man on the ground,

with the savageness of despair. 'If I'm to die let me die alone, not with those devilish eyes of yours watching me!'

By this time the heat was almost unbearable, and Pete's horse was growing unmanageable. He plunged and snorted at the approaching flames, until none but a man of Pete's experience and dexterity could have retained his seat in the saddle.

'Since you do not desire my presence,' said Pete, 'I'll wish you a good afternoon.'

So saying he lifted his hat with diabolical politeness and started for the creek. He had not gone very far, however, before he changed his mind and once more brought his horse to a standstill, this time with even more difficulty than before, for the animal was now almost beyond control. Glancing round to see how far the flames were away, he leapt from the saddle to the ground, and realising that he would not have time to make the beast secure, let him go free, and set off as fast as his legs would carry him back to the spot where he had left his enemy to meet his fate. As he reached it, the flames entered a little belt of timber fifty yards from the place.

'Come, Beeton,' he cried. 'If you're going

to be saved there's not an instant to lose. Let me get a good hold of you and I'll see what I can do. Confound the man, he's fainted.'

Picking the prostrate figure up as if he weighed only a few pounds, he placed him on his shoulder and set off at a run for the creek. It was a race for life with a vengeance, and only a man like Pete could have hoped to win it. As it was, he reached the bank just as the foremost flames were licking up the dry grass not a dozen paces from where he had stood. When they reached the bottom Beeton was saved, but what it was that had induced his benefactor to do it it is doubtful if he himself could tell. That evening, when the fire had passed, he walked into the township and gave himself up to the police, at the same time bidding them send out for the man he had risked his life to save.

I have narrated this incident at some length in order that you may have an idea of the complex character of the man who was later on to exercise such a potent influence on my life. That it was a complex character I don't think anyone will attempt to deny. And it was to those who knew him best that he appeared in the strangest light. How well I remember my first meeting with him.

It was about a month after his arrival in the district that I had occasion one morning to cross the river and visit his selection in order to inquire about a young bull of ours that had been seen working his way down the boundary fence. I rode up to the slip panels, let myself in, and went round the tangled wilderness of green stuff to the back of the house. Much of it was in a tumble-down state ; indeed, I had heard that only three rooms were really habitable. In the yard I found the two black boys previously mentioned, and whom I had had described to me, playing knuckle bones on a log. They looked up at me in some surprise, and when I told one of them to go in and let his master know that I wanted to see him, it was nearly a minute before he did so. In response to the summons, however, Whispering Pete emerged, his queer eyes blinking in the sunlight, for all the world like a cat's. He came over to where I sat on my horse, and asked my business.

'My name is Heggarstone,' I replied. 'And I come from the station across the river. I want to inquire after a young brindle bull that was last seen working his way down your boundary fence. I believe he crossed the river above the township.'

'I don't know that I've seen him,' whispered Pete, at the same time looking into my face and taking stock of me with those extraordinary eyes of his. 'But I'll make inquiries. In the meantime get off your horse and come inside, won't you?'

Anxious to see what sort of place he had made of Merther's old shanty, I got off, and, having made my horse fast to a post, followed Pete into his dwelling. A long and dark passage led from the back door right through the house to the front verandah. Passing along this, we proceeded to a room on the right hand side, the door of which he threw open.

I'd only been in the house once before in my life, and that was when old Merther had the place and kept it like a pig-sty. Now everything was changed, and I found myself in a room such as I had never in my life seen before. It was large and well-shaped, with dark panelled walls, had a big, old-fashioned fireplace at one end, in which half-a-dozen people could have seated themselves comfortably, and a long French window at the other, leading into the verandah, and thence into the tangled wilderness of front garden.

But it was not the shape or the size of the

room that surprised me as much as the way in which it was furnished. Books there were, as in our rooms at home, and to be counted by the hundred, mixed up pell-mell with a collection of antique swords, quite a couple of dozen silver cups on brackets, pictures, a variety of fowling-pieces, rifles and pistols, a couple of suits of armour, looking very strange upon their carved pedestals, an easel draped with a curtain, a lot of what looked like valuable china, a heavy, carved table, two or three comfortable chairs, and last, but by no means least, a piano placed across one corner with a pile of music on the top. Though I had it all before me, I could hardly believe my eyes, for this was the last house in the township I should have expected to find furnished in such a fashion.

'Sit down,' said Pete, pointing to a large chair. 'Perhaps you will let me offer you some refreshment after your ride?'

It was a hot morning, and I was thirsty, so I gladly accepted his hospitality. Hearing this, he went to a quaint old cupboard on one side of the room and from it took a bottle with a gold cap—which I knew contained champagne. This was a luxury of which I had never partaken, for in the bush in those days we were very simple in our tastes, and I doubt if even the grog shanty itself had a bottle of this wine upon the premises, much less any other house in the township. Pete placed two strange-shaped glasses on the table, and then unscrewed the cork, not using a corkscrew as I should have done had I been in his place. The wine creamed and bubbled in the glasses, and, after handing one to me, my host took the other himself, and, bowing slightly, said, 'I drink to our better acquaintance, Mr Heggarstone.'

I knew I ought to say something polite in return, but for the life of me I could think of nothing, so I simply murmured, 'Thank you,' and drank off my wine at a gulp, an action which seemed to surprise him considerably. He said nothing, however, but poured me out another glassful, and then took a small silver case from his pocket which, when he offered it to me, I discovered contained cigarettes.

'Do try one,' he said. 'If you are a cigarette smoker, I think you will enjoy them. They are real Turkish, and as I have them made for myself I can guarantee their purity.'

I took one, lit it, and by the time it was

half smoked felt more at my ease. The wine was having a tranquillising effect upon me, and the strings of my tongue were loosened. I even went so far as to comment upon his room.

'So glad you like it,' he murmured softly, with an intonation impossible to imitate. 'It's so difficult, as possibly you are aware, to make a room in any way artistic in these awful up-country townships—the material one has to work upon is, as a rule, so very, very crude. In this particular instance I can scarcely claim much credit, for this old room was originally picturesque, and all I had to do was to put my things in it, and give them a certain semblance of order.'

'And how do you manage to employ your time up here?' I asked.

He looked at me a little curiously for a moment and then said,—

'Well, in the first place, I have my work among my cattle, and then I paint a little, as you see by that easel, then I have my piano, and my books. But at the same time I feel bound to confess existence is a little monotonous. One wants a friend, you know, and that's why I took the liberty of asking you to come in and see my room.'

Though I did not quite see what my friendship had to do with his room, I could not help feeling a little gratified at the compliment he paid me. Presently I said,—

'I hope you won't think me rude, but would it be too much to ask you to play me something?'

'I will do so with great pleasure,' he answered. 'I am glad you are fond of music. But first let me fill your glass and offer you another cigarette.'

Having made me comfortable, he went across to the piano and sat down before it. For a few moments he appeared to be thinking, and then his fingers fell upon the notes, and a curious melody followed—the like of which I never remember to have heard before. I have always been strangely susceptible to the influence of music, and I think my host must have discovered this, for presently he began to sing in a low, silky sort of voice, that echoed in my brain for hours afterwards. What the song was I do not know, but while it lasted I sat entranced. When it was finished he rose and came across to me again.

'I hope you will take pity upon a poor hermit, and let me see you sometimes,' he said, lighting another cigarette. 'For the future you must consider this house and all it contains yours, whenever you care to use it.'

I took this as a dismissal and accordingly rose, at the same time thanking him for the treat he had given me.

'Oh, please don't be so grateful!' he said, with a laugh, 'or I shall begin to believe you don't mean it. Well, if you really must be going, let me call your horse.'

He opened the door and gave a peculiar whistle, which was immediately answered from the back premises. A few moments later my horse made his appearance before the front verandah. I shook hands, and, having mounted, looked once more into his curious eyes, and then rode away. It was only when I reached home, and my father asked what answer I had brought back, that I remembered I had learned nothing of the animal about which I had ridden over to inquire.

My father said nothing, because there was nothing to be said, but he evidently thought the more. As for me, I could think of nothing but that curious man, and the peculiar fascination he had exercised over me.

A few days later I met him in the township.

Directly he saw me he stopped his horse and entered into conversation with me.

'I have been wondering when I should see you again,' he said. 'I was beginning to be afraid you had forgotten that such a person existed.'

'I have been wanting to come up and see you,' I answered, 'but I did not like to thrust myself upon you. You might have been busy.'

'You need never be afraid of that,' he answered, with his usual queer smile. 'No— please come up whenever you can. I shall always be glad to see you. What do you say to Thursday evening at eight o'clock?'

I answered that I should be very glad to come, and then we separated, and I rode on to see Sheilah.

Thursday evening came, and as soon as I had my supper, I set off across the creek to the old house on the hill. It had struck eight by the time I reached it, and to my surprise I heard the sound of voices coming from the sitting-room. I knocked at the door, and a moment later it was opened by my host himself, who shook me warmly by the hand and invited me to enter. Thereupon I passed into the lamp-lit room to discover two

young men of the township, Pat Doolan and
James Mountain, installed there. They were
making themselves prodigiously at home, as
if they had been there many times before.
Which I believe they had.

'I need not introduce you, I suppose?'
said my host, looking round. 'You are
probably well acquainted with these gentle-
men.'

As I had known them all my life, played
with them as children, and met them almost
every day since, it may be supposed that
I was.

We sat down and a general conversation
ensued. After a while our host played and
sang to us; drinks were served, and later
on somebody—I really forget who—suggested
a game of cards. The pasteboards were accordingly produced, and for the first time in my
life I played for money. When, two hours
later, we rose from the table, I was the winner
of twenty pounds, while Pete had lost nearly
fifty. I went home as happy as a man could
well be, with the world in my watch pocket,
not because I had won the money, but because I had been successful in something I
had undertaken. How often that particular
phase of vanity proves our undoing. Two

evenings later I returned and won again, yet another evening, and still with the same result. Then the change came, my luck broke. I followed it up, but still lost. After that the sum I had won melted away like snow before the mid-day sun, till, on the fifth evening, I rose from the table having lost all I had previously won and fifteen pounds into the bargain. The next night I played again, hoping to retrieve my fortune, but ill-luck still pursued me, and I lost ten pounds more. This time it was much worse, for I had not enough capital by twenty pounds to meet my liabilities. I rose from the table like many another poor fool, bitterly cursing the hour I had first touched a card. The others had gone home, and when I prepared to follow them, Pete, to whom I owed the money, accompanied me into the verandah.

' I'm sorry you've had such bad luck lately,' he said quietly. 'But you mustn't let the memory of the small sum you owe me trouble you. I'm in no hurry for it. Fortune's bound to smile on you again before very long, and then you can settle with me at your convenience.'

'To tell the honest truth,' I blurted out, feeling myself growing hot all over, 'I can't pay. I ought not to have played at all.'

'Oh, don't say that,' he answered. 'Remember we only do it for amusement. If you let your losses worry you I shall be more than miserable. No! come up next Monday evening, and let us see what will happen then.'

Monday night came and I played and won!

I paid Pete, and then, because I was a coward and afraid to stop lest they should laugh at me, began again. Once more I won, then Fortune again began to frown upon me, and I lost. We played every evening after that with varying success. At last the crash came. One evening, after liquidating my liabilities to the other men, I rose from the table owing Whispering Pete a hundred pounds.

Bidding him good-night, I went down the hill in a sort of stupor. How I was to pay him I could not think. I had not a halfpenny in the world, and nothing that I could possibly sell to raise the money. That night, as may be imagined, I did not sleep a wink.

Next morning I asked my father to advance me the amount in question. He inquired my reason, and as I declined to give it, he refused to consider my request.

After that, for more than a week, I kept

away from the house on the hill, being too much ashamed to go near it. My life, from being a fairly happy one, now became a burden to me. I carried my miserable secret locked up in my breast by day, and dreamed of it by night.

Then the climax came. One evening a note from Whispering Pete was brought to me by one of his black boys. I took it into the house and read it with my coward heart in my mouth. It ran as follows :—

'DEAR JIM,—Have you quite forgotten me? I have been hoping every evening that you would come across for a chat. But you never put in an appearance. I suppose you have been too busy mustering lately to have any time to spare for visiting. If you are likely to be at home to-morrow evening, will you come across to supper at eight ?—Yours ever,

'PETE.

'*P.S.*—By the way, would it be convenient to you to let me have that £100? I am sending down to Sydney, and being a trifle short it would just come in handily for a little speculation I have on hand.'

Telling the boy to inform his master that I would come over and see him first thing in the morning, I returned to my own room and went to bed—but not to sleep.

Next morning I saddled my horse and rode over as I had promised. When I arrived at the house, Whispering Pete was in the stable at the rear examining a fine chestnut horse that had just arrived. As soon as he saw me he looked a little confused I thought, and came out, carefully closing the door behind him. From the stable we passed into the house and to the sitting-room, where Pete bade me be seated.

'I was beginning to fear I had offended you in some way, and that you wished to avoid me,' he began, as he offered me a cigarette.

'So I did,' I answered boldly, 'and it's on account of that wretched money. Pete, I'm in an awful hole. I cannot possibly pay you just yet. To tell you the honest truth, at the present moment I haven't a red cent in the world, and I feel just about the meanest wretch in all Australia.'

He gave his shoulders a peculiar twitch, as was his habit, and then rose to his feet, saying as he did so,—

'And so you've worked yourself into this state about a paltry hundred pounds. Well, if I'd been told it by anybody else I'd not have believed it. Come, come, Jim, old man, if that debt worries you, we'll strike it off the books altogether. Thank God, I can safely say I'm not a money-grubber, and, all things considered, I set a greater value on your society than on twice a hundred pounds. So there that's done with, and you must forget all about it!'

Generous as was his speech I could not help thinking there was something not quite sincere about it. However, he had lifted a great weight off my mind, and I thanked him profusely, at the same time telling him I should still regard myself as in his debt, and that I would repay him on the first possible opportunity.

'Would you really like to pay me?' he said suddenly, as if an idea had struck him. 'Because, if you are desirous of doing so, I think I can find you a way by which you can not only liquidate your debt to me, but recoup yourself for all your losses into the bargain.'

'And what is that?' I asked. 'If it's possible, of course I should like to do it.'

'Well, I'll tell you. It's like this! You

know, next month the township races come off, don't you? Well, it's to be the biggest meeting they have ever had, and, seeing that, I have determined to bring up a horse from the South and enter him for the Cup. Now, here's what I propose. I know your reputation as a horseman, and I think with you in the saddle my nag can just about win. I'll pay you a hundred pounds to ride him, and there you are. What do you say?'

I thought for a moment, and then said,—

'I won't take the hundred, but I'll ride the horse for you, if you wish it, with pleasure.'

'Thank you,' he answered.   'I thought I could depend on you.'

Little did I dream to what misery I was condemning myself by so readily consenting to his proposition.

From Whispering Pete's house I went on through the township to see Sheilah. It was a lovely morning, with just a suspicion of a coming thunderstorm in the air. I found her in the yard among her fowls, a pale blue sun-bonnet on her head, and a basket full of eggs upon her arm. She looked incomparably sweet and womanly.

'Why, Jim,' she said, looking up at me as I opened the gate and came into the yard, 'this is, indeed, an unexpected pleasure. I thought you were out mustering in your back country.'

'No, Sheilah,' I replied. 'I had some important business in the township, which detained me. Directly it was completed I thought I'd come over and see you.'

'That was kind of you,' she answered. 'I was wondering when you would come. We don't seem to have seen so much of you lately as we used to do.'

Because there was a considerable amount of truth in what she said, and my conscience pricked me for having forsaken old friends for a new-comer like Whispering Pete, I naturally became indignant at such an accusation being brought against me. Sheilah looked at me in surprise, but for a few moments she said nothing, then, as we left the yard and went up the path towards the house, she put her little hand upon my arm and said softly,—

'Jim, my dear old friend, you've something on your mind that's troubling you. Won't you tell me all about it and let me help you if I can?'

'It's nothing that you can help me in, Sheilah,' I replied. 'I'm down on my luck, that's all; and, because I'm a fool, I've promised to do a thing that I know will make a lot of trouble in the future.   However, as it can't be helped, it's no use crying over it, is it?'

'Every use, if it can make you any nappier.   Jim, you've not been yourself for weeks past.   Come, tell me all about it, and let me see if I can advise you.   Has it, for instance, anything to do with Whispering Pete?'

I looked at her in surprise.

'What do you know about Whispering Pete?' I asked.

'A good deal more than you think, or I like,' she answered, 'and when I find him making my old playfellow miserable, I am even more his enemy than before.'

'I didn't say that it had anything to do with Whispering Pete,' I retorted, beginning to flare up, according to custom, at the idea of anything being said or hinted against those with whom I was intimate.

'No, Jim, you didn't say so, but I'm certain he *is* at the bottom of it, whatever it is!   Come, won't you tell me, old friend?'

She looked into my face so pleadingly that I could not refuse her; besides, it had always been my custom to confide in Sheilah ever since I was a little wee chap but little bigger than herself, and somehow it seemed to come natural now.   What's more, if the truth were known, I think it was just that very idea that had brought me down to see her.

'It's this way, Sheilah,' I stammered, hardly knowing how to begin. 'Like the fool I am, I've been playing cards up at Whispering Pete's for the last month or so, and, well, the long and the short of it is, I've lost more money than I can pay.'

She didn't reproach me, being far too clever for that. She simply put her little hand in mine, and looked rather sorrowfully into my face.

'Well, Jim?' she said.

'Well, to make a long story short, I owe Whispering Pete a hundred pounds. He wrote asking me for the money. I couldn't pay, so I went over and told him straight out that I couldn't.'

'That was brave of you!'

'He received me very nicely and generously, and told me not to bother myself any more about it. Then I found there was something I could do for him in return.'

'And what was that?'

'Why, to ride his horse for the Cup at the township races next month.'

'Oh, Jim—you won't surely do that, will you?'

'Well, you see I've promised, and it's that that's worrying me.'

'Jim, what is the amount you want to pay him off?'

'A hundred pounds, Sheilah.'

'Well, I have more than that saved. Jim, do let me lend it to you, and then you can pay him in full, and you needn't ride in the race. You know, Jim, that nobody among our friends in the township ever goes to them, and you must see for yourself what would be said if you rode.'

'And what business would it be of anybody's pray, if I did? I go my way, they can go theirs.'

'But I don't want people to think badly of you, Jim.'

'If they're fools enough to do so because I ride a good horse in a fair race they'll think anything; and, as far as I'm concerned, they're welcome to their opinions.'

'And you won't let me lend you the money, Jim?'

'No, Sheilah, dear, it's impossible. I couldn't think of such a thing. But I thank you all the same from the bottom of my heart. It's like your goodness to make me such an offer.'

'And you've made up your mind to ride for this man.'

'See for yourself how I am situated. How can I get out of it? He has done me a kindness, and in return he asks me to do him one. If I can't do anything else I can ride, and he is pinning his chance of winning on me. Am I therefore to disappoint him because the old goody-goodies in the township disapprove of horse-racing?'

'Jim, that isn't the right way to look at it.'

'Isn't it? Well, it's the way I've got to look at it anyhow, and, as far as I can see, there's no other. Only, I'll give you one bit of advice, don't let any of the people hereabouts come preaching to me, or they'll find I'm not in the humour for it.'

Sheilah was quiet for a little while. Then she said very sorrowfully,—

'This man's coming into the township will prove to have been the beginning of trouble for all of us. Jim, mark my words; your decision will some day recoil upon those you love best.'

This was not at all what I expected from Sheilah, so like a fool I lost my temper.

'What nonsense you talk,' I cried. 'At any

rate, if it does it will do us good. We want a bit of waking up, or I'm mistaken.'

'Oh, Jim, Jim,' she said, 'if only I could persuade you to give this notion up.'

'It's not to be thought of, Sheilah,' I answered, 'so say no more about it. One thing I know, however, and that is, if all the rest turn against me, you will not.'

'I shall never turn against you, Jim. And you know that.'

'Well, then, that's all right. I don't care a scrap about the rest.

'But does it never strike you, Jim, that in thus following your own inclinations you are being very cruel to those who love you best in the world.'

'Those who love me best in the world,' I repeated mockingly. 'Pray how many may there be of them?'

'More than you seem to think,' she answered reproachfully. 'If only you were not so headstrong and proud, you would soon discover that you have in reality lots of friends—even among those whom you affect to despise. Some day you may find this out. God grant it may not then be too late.'

How true her words were destined to

prove you will see for yourself. Surely enough the time *was* to come, the bitterest time of all my life, when I should see for myself in what estimation I was held by the people of the township. Strange are the ways of Providence, for then it was I discovered that my best friends were not those who had been my companions in prosperity, and whom I had every right to think would stand by me through evil and good report — but the very people whom I had been accustomed to call *old fossils* and by a hundred other and similar terms of reproach. However, I was not going to give in that Sheilah was right.

'Too late or not too late,' I answered, 'I must go my own way, Sheilah. If it turns out that I'm wrong, I shall have to suffer for my folly. If I'm beaten, you may be sure I sha'n't cry out. I'll take my punishment like a man, never fear. I'll not ask anyone to share my punishment.'

She gave a little sigh.

'No, you're not asking us to share your punishment,' she replied. 'Nevertheless we must do so. Can you not think and see for yourself what it must mean to those who are your friends and have your welfare most at heart, to see you so blindly thrusting your head into the trap that is so cunningly set for you by the arch enemy of all mankind?'

'How do you know it *is* a trap?' I cried. 'Why will you always make such mountains out of molehills, Sheilah? If, as you say, Pete is my enemy, which, mind you, I do not for a single moment admit, he cannot do me very much harm. I may lose a little money to him at cards, but I shall soon be able to pay him back. I may ride his horse for him at the township races and offend some of the strait-laced goody-goody folk by so doing—but their censure will break no bones, and in a few weeks they will have forgotten it and be much the same to me as ever. It is not as if I were going to continue race riding all my life, because I do it this once. I may never ride another. Indeed, I'll even go so far as to give you my promise to that effect if you wish it.'

'You will make me very happy if you will.'

'Then I'll do so,' I answered. 'From this moment I promise you that, without your permission, I will never ride another horse in a race. There! Are you satisfied now?'

'I am much happier. I thank you, Jim, from the bottom of my heart. For I know you well enough to be sure that if you have once given your word you will stick to it. God bless you.'

'God bless you, Sheilah. And now I must be off. Good-bye.'

'Good-bye.'

I jumped on to my horse, and, waving my hand to her, went back up the track to the township with a strange foreboding in my heart that her prophecy would some day be realised.

CHAPTER IV

THE RACE

SLOWLY the month rolled by, and every day brought the fatal races nearer, till at last only a week separated us from them. With each departing day a greater nervousness took possession of me. I tried to reason it out, but without success. As far as I could see, I had nothing very vital to fear! I might lose the esteem of the grey heads of the township, it was true, and possibly get into trouble with my father—but beyond those two unpleasantnesses I was unable to see that anything serious could happen to me.

Since giving him my promise I had only once set eyes on Whispering Pete. To tell the truth, I felt a desire to keep out of his way. At the same time, however, I had not the very slightest intention of going back on my promise to ride for him. At last, one morning, I met him riding through the township on a skittish young thoroughbred. As usual he was scrupulously neat in his dress, and, when he stopped to speak to me, his beady black eyes shone down on me like two live coals.

'You're not going to throw me over about that race are you, Jim?' he said, after we had pulled up our horses and saluted each other.

'What should make you think so?' I answered. 'When I give my word I don't go back on it as a general rule.'

'Of course, you don't,' he replied; 'I know that. But I heard yesterday that the folk in the township had been trying to persuade you to withdraw your offer. The time is drawing close now, and I shall have the horse up here to-night. Come over in the evening and have a look at him, and then in the morning, if you're agreeable and have nothing better to do, we might try him against your horse Benbow, who, I take it, is the best animal in the district. What do you say?'

'I'm quite willing,' I answered. 'And where do you intend to do it?'

'Not where all the township can see, you may be sure,' he answered, with one of his peculiar laughs. 'We'll keep this little affair dark. Do you know that bit of flat on the other side of Sugarloaf Hill?'

'Quite well,' I said. 'Who should know it better than I?'

'Very well, then; we'll have our trial spin there.' Then bending towards me he said very softly, 'Jim, my boy, it won't be my fault if we don't make a big haul over this race. There will be a lot of money about, and you've no objection, I suppose?'

'None whatever,' I answered. 'But do you think it's as certain as all that? Remember it's a pretty stiff course, and from what I heard this morning, the company your horse is likely to meet will be more than usually select.'

'I'm not the least afraid,' he answered. 'My horse is a good one, and if he is well, will walk through them as if they were standing still. Especially with you on his back.'

I took this compliment for what it was worth, knowing that it was only uttered for the sake of giving me a bit of a fillip.

'I shall see you, then, this evening?' I said.

'This evening. Can you come to dinner?'

'I'm afraid not,' I answered; and with a parting salutation we separated and rode on our different ways.

When I reached the corner I turned and looked back at him, asking myself what there was about Whispering Pete that made him so different to other men. That he *was* different nobody could deny. Even the most commonplace things he did and said had something about them that made them different from the same things as done and said by other people. I must confess that, while I feared him a little, I could not help entertaining a sort of admiration for the man. Who and what was he? He had been in the township now, off and on, for two years, and during the whole of that time, with the exception of myself and a few other young men, he had made no friends at all. Indeed, he used to boast that he had no sympathy with men above a certain age, and it was equally certain that not one of the elderly inhabitants of the town, from my father and old McLeod downwards, had any sympathy or liking for him.

When I had watched him out of sight, I rode on to the McLeods' selection, and, having tied up my horse, entered the house. Sheilah, I discovered, was not at home, having ridden out to their back boundary to see a woman who was lying ill at one of the huts. Old McLeod was in the stock-yard, branding some heifers, and I strolled out to give him a hand. When we had finished we put away the irons, and went up the path to the house together. On reaching the dining-room, a neat and pretty room, with Sheilah's influence showing in every corner of it, the old man turned and put his hand on my shoulder. He was a strange-looking old chap, with his long, thin face, bushy grey eyebrows, shaven upper lip, and enormous white beard. After looking at me steadily for a minute or so, he said, with the peculiar Scotch accent that time had never been able to take away from him,—

'James, my lad, it is my business to warn ye to be verra careful what ye're about, for I ken, unless ye mend your ways, ye're on the straight road to hell. And, my boy, I like ye too well to see ye ganging that way without a word to so stay ye.'

'And what have you heard about me, Mr McLeod?' I asked, resolved to have it out with him while the iron was hot. 'What gossip has been carried to your ears?'

'Nay! nay!' he answered. 'Not gossip, my laddie. What I have heard is the sober truth, and that ye'll ken when I tell ye. First an' foremost, ye've been card-playing up at the house on the hill yonder these many months past.'

'That's quite true,' I replied. 'But I can also tell you that I have not seen or touched a card for close upon five weeks now; and, if I can help it, I never will do so again. What else have you been told about me?'

'Well, lad,' he said, 'I've heard that ye're going to ride in the races out on the plain yonder next week. Maybe that'll not be true, too?'

'Yes. It's quite true; I am.'

'But ye'll think better of it, laddie. I'm sure of that!'

'No! I have no option. I have promised to ride, and I cannot draw back.'

'And ye'll have reckoned what the consequences may be?'

'I think I have!'

'Well, well; I'm sorry for ye. Downright sorry, laddie. I thought ye had more strength of mind than that. However, it's no care of mine; ye'll have your own day of reckoning I make no doubt.'

'I cannot see that what I do concerns anyone but myself,' I answered hotly.

He looked at me under his bushy eyebrows for a second or two, and then said, shaking his old head,—

'Foolish talk—vain and verra foolish talk!'

By this time my temper, never one of the best, as you already know, had got completely out of my control, and I began to rage and storm against those who had spoken against me to him, at the same time crying out against the narrowness and hypocrisy of the world in general. Old McLeod gravely heard me to the end, visibly and impartially weighing the pros and cons of all I said. Then, when I had finished, he remarked,—

'Ye're but a poor, half-baked laddie, after all, to run your head against a wall in this silly fashion. But ye'll see wisdom some day. By that time, however, 'twill be too late.'

Never has a prophecy been more faithfully fulfilled than that one. I have learned wisdom since then—learned it as few men have done, by the hardest and bitterest experience. And when I got it, it was, as he had said, too late to be of any use to me. But as that has all to be told in its proper order, I must get on with my story.

Leaving the house, I mounted my horse again and rode off in the direction I knew Sheilah would come, my heart all the time raging within me against the injustice of which I considered myself the victim. What right had old McLeod to talk to me in such a fashion? I was not his son; and, poor fool that I was, I told myself that if I liked I would go to a thousand races and ride in every one of them, before I would consider him or anyone else in the matter. But one thing puzzled me considerably, and that was how he had come to know so much of my private affairs. Since it had been kept such a profound secret, who could have told him about my gambling, and my promise to ride Pete's horse in the steeplechase? So far as I was aware, no one but Sheilah knew, to whom I had told my whole story. Could she have revealed my shortcomings to her father? In my inmost heart, I knew that she had not said a word. But I was so angry that I could not do justice to anybody, not even to Sheilah herself. God help me!

For an hour I rode on ; then, crossing a bit of open plain, I saw Sheilah ahead, mounted on a big brown horse, coming cantering towards me. When she made out who I was, she quickened her pace, and we were presently alongside each other, riding back together. Angry as I was, I could not help noticing how pretty her face looked under her big hat, and how well she sat her horse.

'You seem put out about something, Jim,' she said, when I had turned my horse and we had gone a few yards.

'I am,' I answered, 'very much put out. Sheilah, why did you tell your father what I told you the other day?'

'What have I told him?'

'Why, about my playing cards at Whispering Pete's, and my resolve to ride in the steeplechase next week?'

'I have not told him, Jim. You surely don't think I would be as mean as that, do you?'

'But how did he come to hear of it?' I asked, ignoring the last portion of her speech.
'He taxed me with it this morning, and was

kind enough to preach me a sermon on the strength of it.'

'I have not said a word to him. You seem to have a very poor opinion of me, Jim.'

'You must admit that it's strange he should have known!'

'Don't you think he may have heard it in the township?'

'Your father's not given to gossiping among the township folk; you know that as well as I do, Sheilah!'

'Then you still think, in spite of what I have told you, that I did tell him? Answer me, straightforwardly, do you think so?'

'If you want it in plain English, without any beating about the bush, I do! There, now I have said it.'

For a moment her face flushed crimson, then her eyes filled with tears and she looked another way, thinking I should not see them. As soon as I had spoken I would have given all I possessed in the world to have recalled those fatal words; but my foolish pride would not let me say anything. Then Sheilah turned to me with a white face.

'I am sorry, Jim,' she said slowly, 'that you should think so badly of me as to believe me capable of telling you a lie. God forgive you for doubting one who would be, if you would only let her, your truest and best friend on earth.'

Then giving her horse a smart cut with her whip, she set off at a gallop, leaving me behind, feeling just the meanest and most contemptible cur on earth. For two pins I would have made after her, and licked the very dust off her boots in apology. But before I could do so my temper got the better of me again, and I turned off the track, made for the river, and, having forded it, rode home, about as miserable a man as could have been found in the length and breadth of Australia.

When I reached the house it was hard upon sundown, and old Betty was carrying in dinner. I turned my horse into the night paddock, hung my saddle and bridle on the peg in the verandah, and then went inside. The old woman met me in the passage, and one glance at my face told her what sort of state I was in. She drew me into the kitchen in her old affectionate way, and, having got me there, said,—

'Jim, boy, it's ye that must be very careful to-night. Your father's been at his old tricks all day, and he's just quarrelsome enough now to snap your head off if you say a word. Don't cross him, lad, whatever you do.'

'All right, old girl,' I answered, patting her weather-beaten cheek, and going past her into my room. Then, having changed my things, I went into the dining-room, where my father was sitting with a book upon his knee, staring straight before him.

He looked up as I entered, and shut his volume with a snap; but for some time he did not utter a word, indeed it was not until our meal was well nigh finished that he spoke. Then he put down his knife and fork, poured himself out some whiskey, drank it slowly, with his eyes fixed on me all the time, and said,—

'Pray, what is the meaning of this new scandal that I hear about you?'

'What new scandal?' I asked; for I did not know what false yarn he might have picked up.

'This story about your having promised to ride a horse in the steeplechase next week?'

'It is perfectly true that I have promised,' I answered. 'What more do you want me to tell you about it?'

'I won't tell you what I want you to tell me. I'll tell you what I command, and that is that you don't as much as put your leg over any horse at those races.'

'And, pray, why not?'

He filled himself another glass of whiskey and sipped it slowly.

'Because I forbid it at once and for all. That's why!'

'It's too late to forbid it now. I have given my promise, and I cannot draw back.'

'You both can and will,' he said hotly. 'I order you to.'

'I am sorry,' I answered, trying hard to keep my temper. 'But I have no option. I *must* ride.'

He staggered to his feet, and stood for a moment glaring down at me, his fingers twitching convulsively as he rested them on the table.

'Listen to my last word, you young dog,' he cried. 'I tell you this on my word of honour. If you ride that horse, you leave my house there and then. As surely as you disobey me, I'll have no more to do with you.'

I rose to my feet and faced him. My whole future was trembling in the balance. Little I cared, however.

'Then, if I understand my position aright, I am to choose between your house and my word of honour. A pretty choice for a father to give his son, I must say.'

'Don't dare to bandy words with me, sir!' he cried. 'Take your choice. Give up that race, or no longer consider this your home. That's all I have to say to you. Now go.'

I left the room and went out into the yard. Then, leaning upon the slip rails of the horse paddock, I reviewed the situation. My world was toppling about my ears. I had quarrelled with old McLeod, I had plainly told Sheilah that I disbelieved her, and now I was being called upon to break my plighted word to Pete or lose my home. A nice position I was in, to be sure. Look at it how I would, I could come to no decision more plain than that, in persisting in my determination to ride, I was doing what is generally called cutting off my nose to spite my face. On the other hand, I had given my word, and was in honour bound to Pete. On the other I—but there, what did it all matter; if they could be obstinate, so could I, and come what might I would not give in—no, not if I had to resign all I possessed and go out into the world and begin life again as a common station hand. It's all very well now to say what a fool I was. You must remember I was young, I was hot-headed, and as if that were not enough, I came of a race that

were as vile-tempered as even the Tempter
of Mankind could wish.

After a while I crossed the creek and
went up the hill to Whispering Pete's abode.
I found him in his verandah, smoking. As
soon as he saw me he rose and shook hands.
One glance at my face must have told him
that something was wrong, for he immediately
said,—

'You look worried, Jim. What's the
matter?'

'Everything,' I answered. 'My promise
to ride that horse for you has got me into
a rare hot-bed of trouble.'

'I'm sorry for that,' he replied, offering
me one of his splendid cigars, and pushing
up a chair for me. 'But never mind, you're
going to win a pot of money, and that will
make them forgive and forget, or I don't
know my world. I've got the weights to-
day. My horse has to carry twelve stone.
What do you ride?'

'A little under eleven,' I answered.

'Then that should make it about right.
However, we'll arrange all that to-morrow.'

'Has the horse arrived yet?'

'No,' he answered. 'But I'm expecting
him every minute.'

For a while we chatted on, then suddenly my host sat upright, and bent his head forward in a listening attitude.

'What do you hear?' I asked, for I could only distinguish the rustling of the night wind in the leaves of the creepers that covered the verandah.

'I thought I heard a strange horse's step,' he answered, still listening. 'Yes, there it is again. I expect it's my animal arriving.'

A few moments later I could plainly distinguish the clatter of a horse's step on the hard beaten track that led up to the door. How Pete had heard it so long before I could not imagine. Presently a dark form appeared against the starlight, and pulled up opposite where we sat. Pete sprang to his feet and went forward to the steps.

'Is that you, Dick?' he cried.

'My word, it is,' came back a voice from the darkness. 'And a nice job I've had of it.'

'Well, then, follow the track round to the left there, and I'll meet you at the stables.'

The horseman did as he was ordered, and when he had disappeared, Pete turned to me and said,—

'If you would care to see the horse, come with me.'

I accordingly rose and followed him through the house to the back regions. When we reached the stables we found the stranger dismounted and in the act of leading a closely - rugged horse into a loose - box, which had evidently been specially prepared for his reception. Pete followed him, and said something in a low voice, to which the man, who was a tall, weedy individual, murmured some reply. Having done so, he spat on the floor with extreme deliberation, and wiped his mouth on his sleeve.

'Now, let us have a look at him,' said Pete, signing to a blackboy to strip him of his clothing. The boy did as he was ordered, and for the first time I saw the horse whose destiny it was to change the whole course of my life.

He was a fine-looking, bright bay, with black points, standing about fifteen hands, long and low, with short, flat legs, large, clean hocks, good thighs, and as sweet a head and neck as any man ever saw on a horse. Long as was the stage he had evidently done that day, he looked as fresh as paint as his big eyes roamed about and took in the lamp-lit box which was ever so much below what a beauty of his kind deserved. Somehow it seems to come natural to every Australian, man or woman, to be a lover of a good horse, and I know that, as I looked at that beautiful beast, all my regrets were forgotten and my whole soul rose in longing to be upon his back.

'What do you think of him?' said Pete, who had been closely watching my face. 'Isn't he a beauty, and doesn't he look as if he ought to be able to show the animals about here the way to go?'

'He does, indeed,' I answered. 'But don't you think it seems a waste of good material to bring a horse like that up here to take part in a little country race meeting.'

'I want to show the folk about here what I can do, my boy,' he said, and dropping his voice lower even than usual, he continued, 'Besides, as I told you to-night, the race will be worth more than a little. Between ourselves, I stand to win five thousand over it already, and if you've got any savee you'll have a bit on him, especially as you're going to ride him yourself, and therefore know it must all be fair, square, and above board.

I intend, all being well, to back him as far as my means will permit,' I said. 'And now, with regard to this trial, is that to come off to-morrow morning?'

'No! I think not. The horse is not ready for it. The day after to-morrow, perhaps, at three in the morning, on the flat behind the Sugarloaf Hill. Is old Benbow anything like well?'

'As fit as possible,' I said. 'If your horse can give him a stone, I shall be quite satisfied.'

'Well, bring him over and we'll try. The result should give us some idea of how this chap can go.'

'By the way, you've never told me his name.'

'He is called The Unknown, if that tells you anything.'

'Not much,' I answered, at the same time giving a final glance at the beautiful animal now undergoing his toilet. He had only one blemish as far as I could see, and I had to look him over pretty closely to find it, and that was a small, white mark on the point of the bone of his near hock. It caught the eye, and, as I thought, looked unsightly. Just as we were leaving the box, Pete, who was behind me, suddenly stopped, and turned angrily on the man sponging the horse's legs,

'You clumsy fool,' he cried, 'are you quite without sense? One more piece of forgetfulness like that and you'll spoil everything.'

What it was that he complained of I could not say, for when I turned round he was carefully examining the horse's off fore knee, but the man he addressed looked woefully distressed.

'Attend to that at once,' said Pete, with an ugly look upon his face. 'And let me catch you neglecting your duties again, and I'll call in the One-eyed Doctor to you. Just you remember that.'

Then taking my arm, Pete drew me across the yard back to the house. There I took a glass of grog, and, after a little conversation, bade him good-bye.

It was a lovely night when I left the house and started for home. A young moon lay well down upon the opposite hilltop, and her faint light sparkled on the still water of the creek. Now and again a night bird hooted in the scrub, and once or twice 'possums ran across and scuttled up into the trees to right and left of my path. My thoughts were still full of my awkward position, but I would not alter my determination a jot; I had only one regret, and that was my conduct towards Sheilah.   From the place where I stood by the ford I could see the light of her bedroom window shining distinctly as a star down the valley.   I watched it till my eyes ached, then, with a heavy sigh, continued my walk up the hill, and, having reached the house, went straight to bed.

On the morning appointed for the trial I was up before it was light, had saddled old Benbow, whom I had kept in the stable for two days, so that he might be the fitter for the work which would be required of him, and was at the Sugarloaf Hill just as the first signs of dawn were making their appearance.   I had not long to wait before the others put in an appearance—Pete mounted on the handsome black I have elsewhere described, and the man he had called Dick on The Unknown.   We greeted each other, and then set to work arranging preliminaries.

'You had better get on The Unknown, Jim,' said Pete, 'and let Dick, here, ride Benbow.   I'll give you a lead for the first half of the distance, then Dick can pick you up and take you on to the end.   That should tell us pretty well what the horse can do, I think.'

I changed places with the man, and for the first time realised what a compact horse The Unknown was. The course was then pointed out to me, and the groom went on to his place to wait for us. The sun was just in the act of rising, and already the magpies were making day musical in the trees above us. A heavy dew lay upon the grass, and the air was as cool and fresh as the most luxurious could desire.

'Now,' said Pete, gathering up his reins preparatory to business, 'when you're ready we'll start.'

'I'm quite ready,' I said, taking my horse in hand.

With that we walked back a yard or two, and turned round. No sooner had we done so than Pete cried, 'Go!' As the word left his lips the two horses sprang forward and away we went. The wind whistled and shrieked past our ears—the trees and shrubs came into view and fell behind us like objects seen from the windows of an express train—but I was only conscious of the glory of the gallop and the exquisite action of the beast beneath me   By the time we had picked up

Benbow, Pete's horse was done. Then I took the other horse on, and at the appointed tree had beaten him easily, with a couple of lengths to spare. After that I gradually eased him down and returned to the others, his head in the air, his ears pricked, and his feet dancing upon the earth as if he were shod with satin instead of steel.

'What do you think of him now that you've tried him?' said Pete, as I came back to where he and his companion were standing waiting for me.

'I think he's as good as he's handsome,' I replied enthusiastically, 'and if he doesn't make the company he is to meet next week sing small — well — I don't know anything about horses.'

'Let us hope he will. Now, Dick, change saddles and then take him home, and be sure you look after him properly.'

The animal and his rider having disappeared round the hill, we mounted our horses again and made our way back to the river. As we went Pete gave me an outline of the scheme he had arranged for backing his horse. I had understood all along that he intended to make it a profitable speculation, but I had no idea it was as big as he gave me to understand it was.

At last the day before the races arrived. For nearly a week before the township had been assuming a festive garb. The three hotels, for the one grog shanty I have mentioned as existing at the time of the Governor's visit so many years before, had now been relegated to a back street, and three palatial drinking-houses, with broad verandahs, bars, and elegant billiard and dining-rooms, had grown up along the main street, were crammed with visitors. Numbers of horsey - looking men had arrived by coach from the nearest railway terminus, a hundred miles distant, and the various stables of the township were filled to overflowing. The race week was an event of great importance in our calendar, and, though the more sober-minded of the population professed to strongly disapprove of it, the storekeepers and hotelkeepers found it meant such an increase of business, that for this reason they encouraged its continuance. The racecourse itself was situated across the creek, and almost directly opposite the McLeod's selection. It consisted of a plain of considerable size, upon which the club had made a nice track with a neat grand stand, weighing-shed, saddling - paddock, and ten pretty stiff jumps.

I rose early on the morning of Cup Day, and had finished my breakfast before my father was out of bed. I had no desire to risk an encounter with him, so I thought I would clear out before he was astir. But I was bargaining without my host; for just as I was setting off for the township, he left his room and came out into the verandah.

'Of course you know what you're doing,' he called to me.

I answered that I did.

'Well, remember what I told you,' he replied. 'As certainly as you ride that horse to-day, I'll turn you out of my house to-night. Make no mistake about that!'

'I quite understand,' I answered. 'I've given my word to ride and I can't go back on it. If you like to punish me for keeping my promise and acting like a gentleman, well, then, you must do so. But I'll think no more of you for it, and so I tell you!'

'Ride that horse and see what I'll do,' he shouted, shaking his fist at me, and then disappeared into his room. I did not wait for him to come out again, but went down the track whistling to keep my spirits up. Having crossed the creek I made my way up the hill to Whispering Pete's house, reaching it in time to find him at breakfast with a man I had never seen before. The first view I had of this individual did not prepossess me in his favour.

His hair was black as—well, as black as Pete's eyes—but his face was deathly pale, with the veins showing up blue and matted on either temple. To add still further to his curious appearance, he had but one eye and one arm. The socket of the eye that was missing gaped wide, and almost made one turn away in disgust. But his voice was, perhaps, the most extraordinary thing about him. It was as soft and caressing as a woman's, and every time he spoke he gave you the idea he was trying to wheedle something out of you.

Pete rose and introduced him to me as Dr Finnan, of Sydney, and when we had shaken hands I sat down at the table with them. The Doctor asked me my opinion of the season, the prospects of the next wool clip, my length of residence in the district, and finally came round to what I knew he was working up to all the time—namely, my opinion of my chance in the race to be run that day. I answered that, having considered the various horses engaged I thought I could just about win, and on inquiry, learnt that the animal I was to ride had not started for the course, and would not do so until just before the time of the race.

'And I commend your decision,' said the Doctor, sweetly; 'he is a nervous beast, and the turmoil of a racecourse could only tend to disturb his temper.'

After breakfast we sat and smoked for perhaps half-an-hour, and were in the act of setting off for the racecourse, when a boy rode up to the verandah and called to Pete to know if I were inside. On being informed that I was, he took a note from his cabbage-tree hat and handed it to me. It was from Sheilah, and ran as follows :—

'DEAR OLD JIM, — Is it too late for your greatest friend to implore you not to ride to-day? I have a feeling that if you do, it will bring misery upon both of us. You know how often my prophecies come true. At any hazard, give it up, I implore you, and make happy—Your sincere friend,

'SHEILAH.

I crushed the note in my fingers, and told the boy to say there was no answer. It was too late to draw back now.

Nevertheless, I felt I would have given anything I possessed to have been able to do what Sheilah asked.

A little before twelve we left the house and went down the path to the township, crossed the river at the ferry, and walked thence to the course. Already numbers of people were making their way in the same direction, while more were flocking in from the district on the other side. The course itself, when we reached it, presented an animated appearance with its booths and lines of carriages, and by the time we entered the grand stand enclosure the horses were parading for the first race. That once over we lunched, and then I went off to the tent set apart for the jockeys, to dress. Pete's colours consisted of a white jacket with black bars and a red cap, and I found one of his blackboys waiting with them at the door.

As soon as I was ready I took my saddle and bridle and went down to the weighing-shed in the saddling-paddock. Then, on my weight being declared 'correct,' set off in search of Pete and the horse. I found them under a big gum-tree putting the final touches to the toilet of an animal I scarcely recognised. Since I had last seen him a few important changes had been made in his appearance; his mane had been hogged and his tail pulled a good deal shorter than it was before. What was more, the peculiar white spot on his hock had been painted out, for not a sign of it could I discover though I looked pretty hard for it. I was about to ask the reason of his altered appearance when the bell sounded, and the Doctor cried,—

'All aboard. There's no time to lose. Be quick, Mr Heggarstone.'

Pete gave me a lift, and I settled myself comfortably in the saddle. Then gathering up my reins I made my way into the straight. As I passed the scratching board I glanced at it, and saw that three competitors were missing; this left eight runners. One thing, however, surprised me; the Unknown was only quoted at eight to one in the betting ring — the favourite being a well-known Brisbane mare, Frivolity by name. The Emperor, a big chestnut gelding, and Blush Rose, a bonny little mare, were also much fancied. Nobody seemed to know anything at all of my mount.

After the preliminary canter, we passed through a gate in the railings on the opposite

side of the straight, and assembled about a
hundred yards below the first fence. I was
second from the outside on the left, a big
grey horse, named Lochinvar, being on my
right, and Frivolity on my left. There was
a little delay in starting, caused by the
vagaries of Blush Rose, who would not
come into line. Then the starter dropped
his flag, and away we went. For the first
hundred yards or so it was as much as
I could do to keep my horse in hand; indeed, by the time I had got him steadied
we were in the quadruple enclosure, charg-
ing in a mass at the first fence, a solid
wall of logs placed on top of each other.
Blush Rose and a big bay named Highover,
ridden by a well-known Brisbane professional,
were the first to clear it. I came third,
with the Emperor close alongside me.
Where we left the ground on taking off
and where we landed on the other side I
have no notion. I only know that we *did*
get over, that the big post and rail fence
came next, and that after that we raced
at the stone wall. At the latter two horses
fell, and by the time we reached the other
side of the course, opposite the stand, two
more had followed suit. When we reached

the quadruple again our number had dwindled down to three — The Emperor, Blush Rose, and The Unknown. Then as we passed through the gate in the quadruple picket fence, the rider of The Emperor challenged me, and we went at the logs together neck and neck. The result was disastrous; my horse took off too soon, hit it with his chest and turned a complete somersault, throwing me against the rails. I could not have been on the ground more than a minute, however, before I was up again, feeling as sick as a dog, and looking for my horse. A man had caught him and was holding him for me. Hardly knowing how I did it, I scrambled into the saddle and set off again in pursuit of the others. It seemed at first impossible that I could overtake them, but I was always hard to beat, and gradually I began to draw a wee bit closer. Little by little I decreased the distance until, at last, I was only a few lengths behind them.

In spite of the distance he had had to make up The Unknown was still full of running, so as fast as our horses could lay their legs to the ground we rode at the last fence. With a blind rush the trio rose into the air together, and came safely down on the other side. Then on we went, amid a hurricane of cheers, past the stand, between the two lines of carriages, and towards the judge's box. I have but an imperfect recollection of the last hundred yards. I was only conscious that Blush Rose was alongside me, that we were neck and neck, and that we were both doing all we knew. Then, as we approached the box, I lifted my whip and called upon my horse for a last effort. He responded gamely, and half-a-dozen strides later I had landed him winner by a neck.

CHAPTER V

CONSEQUENCES

As soon as I reached the scales after the race, and had dismounted and weighed, Pete pushed his way through the crowd and clapped his hand upon my shoulder.

'A beautiful race,' he cried enthusiastically, 'and splendidly ridden. You eclipsed even yourself, Jim. Now you must come along with me and let us drink your health.'

I wanted a stimulant pretty badly, for my fall had been a severe one, and I was still feeling dizzy from it. So I followed him to the booth at the back of the grand stand, where I found the One-eyed Doctor and another man, whom I had never seen before, awaiting our coming in close conversation. The stranger was a medium-sized, sandy-haired person, with mutton-chop whiskers and sharp, twinkling eyes. He might have been a member of any profession from a detective to a bookmaker. His name was Jarman, and when I came up he was good enough to congratulate me on winning my race. Then, turning to Pete, he said quietly,—

'By the way, there's something I've been meaning to ask you for the last half-hour. How's your horse bred?'

Pete seemed surprised for a second, then he quickly recovered himself and answered,—

'Don't ask me, for I'm sure I couldn't tell you. I picked him up, quite by chance, out of a likely-looking mob from the South. He may be well bred, he certainly looks it, but, on the other hand, he may not, so as I shall soon sell him again, and don't want to tell any lies about it, I think it safest not to inquire; you can see his brand for yourself.'

Then two or three more men came up, and we had another, and yet another, round of drinks, till I began to feel as if, after all my excitement, I had had more than was prudent. But somehow I didn't care. I was desperate, and drink seemed to drive the blue devils away! I knew that by riding the race I had done for myself, lock, stock, and barrel, so far as my own prospects were concerned, so what did anything else matter. At last it was time to start for home.

'By the way, Mr Jarman,' said Pete, turning to the man who had asked the question about the horse's breeding, 'if you've nothing better to do this evening, won't you come up to my place to dinner. You'll join us, Jim?'

I jumped at the opportunity—for I was certainly not going home, to be insulted and shown the door by my father. Jarman accepted the invitation with companionable alacrity, and then the four of us set off together for the township. By the time we reached it my head was swimming with the liquor I had taken, and I have only a very confused recollection of what followed. I know that we sat down to dinner, waited on by one of the blackboys; I know that I drank every time anything was offered to me, and that I talked incessantly; I am also horribly aware that, do what I would, I could not drive the picture of poor little Sheilah's troubled face out of my brain. I also recollect seeing Jarman sitting opposite me with his impassive, yet always closely-observant face, listening to everything that was said, and watching Pete continually. Great as had been my success that day, and triumphant as I naturally felt at winning the race—I think that that was the most ghastly meal of which I have ever partaken. At last an idea seized me, why or wherefore I cannot tell, and would not be denied. It urged me to go home and get my trouble with my father over. I staggered to my feet, and as I did so the whole room seemed to reel and fall away from me. Feeling like a criminal going to execution, I bade them all good night. Pete looked at me with a queer, half-contemptuous smile upon his face, and I noticed that Jarman rose as if he were going to stop me, but evidently changed his mind and sat down again in his chair. Then reeling out into the verandah, I picked my way carefully down the steps, and set off for my home.

How I managed to get there I cannot say, for my rebellious legs would not, or could not, carry me straight for three yards on end. But at last I managed it, and went boldly up the steps into the front verandah. Nobody was there, so I passed into the dining-room, where a lamp was burning brightly. Pushing my way round the chairs, I came to a standstill before the table and confronted my father, who sat in the furthest corner with a book upon his knee as usual. He looked up at me, and I looked down at him. Then he said very calmly, 'Well, what do you want here?'

I tried to speak, but my voice failed me.

'You rode the horse in spite of my orders to the contrary, I suppose?'

'I did,' I answered—my poor head swimming all the time.

'And I suppose, having defied me to the very best of your ability, you have come back expecting me to forget and forgive?'

'I do not expect anything,' I stammered; 'I only want to know what you intend doing with me. That's all.'

'Well, that's easily told,' he answered. 'Of course I intend sticking to my share of the bargain. As I warned you, you leave this house to-night, and until I ask you, you'd better not come near it again.'

'And then you can ask as long as you please and you'll find I won't come,' I replied. 'No, no! You needn't be afraid of my troubling you. My home has not been made so sweet to me that I should love it so devotedly. You've been an unnatural father to me all my life, and this is the only logical outcome of it.'

He pointed furiously to the door, and without another word I took the hint and left the room. Then I fumbled my way across the verandah down into the garden, and having reached it, stopped to look back at the house. My father was now standing on the steps watching me. His head was bare, and his grey hair was just stirred by the cool night wind. I held on to a post of the wire fence, and looked at him. Seeing that I did not go away he shook his fist at me, and dared me to come back on peril of my life; assuring me with an oath that he would shoot me like a dog if I ever showed my face in his grounds again. There was something so devilish about the old man's anger, that I was more afraid of him than I should have been of a young man twice his size and strength, so I said no more, but went back on my tracks down the hill, over the ford, and up again to Whispering Pete's. It was as if Pete were deliberately drawing me towards the tragedy that was to prove the undoing of all my life.

Reaching the house, I stumbled up the steps on to the verandah. I had not been gone more than three-quarters of an hour, but it seemed like years. Remembering all that had happened to me in the interval, it came almost like a shock to me to find Pete, the One-eyed Doctor and Jarman still seated at the table, conversing as quietly as when

I had left them. The room was half full of smoke, and it was to be easily seen that they had been drinking more than was good for them. I can recall Pete's evil face smiling through the cigar smoke even now.

As my footsteps sounded in the verandah Jarman rose to his feet and, putting his hand on Pete's shoulder, said, in a loud voice, 'In the Queen's name, I arrest you, Peter Dempster, and you, Edward Finnan, on a charge of horse-stealing.' For upwards of a minute there was complete silence in the room. Then Pete turned half round, and, quick as a cat, sprang at Jarman, who had stepped back against the wall. There was a wild struggle that scarcely lasted more than half-a-dozen seconds, then Pete forced his antagonist into a chair, and, while holding him by the throat, picked up a knife from the table, drove it into his breast, plucked it out, and drove it in again. The blood spurted over his hands, and Jarman, feeling his death agony upon him, gave a great cry for help that rang far out into the dark night. Then there was silence again, broken only by a horrible kind of choking noise from the body on the chair, and the hooting of a mopoke in the tree above the house. Try how I would I could not move from the place where I stood, until Pete sprang to his feet and put the knife down on a plate, taking particular care that it should not touch the white linen cloth. The meticulous precision of his action gave me back my power of thinking, and what was more, sobered me like a cold douche. What should I do? What could I do? But there was no time for anything—I must have moved and made a noise, for suddenly the Doctor, revolver in hand, sprang to the window and threw it open, discovering me.

'You!' he cried, as soon as he became aware of my identity. 'My God! you can thank your stars it's you. Come inside.'

Almost unconsciously I obeyed, and stepped into the room. Pete was at the further end, examining his finger. He looked up at me, licking his thin lips, cat fashion, as he did so.

'Damn it all, I've cut my finger,' he said, as coolly as if he had done it paring his nails.

'For pity's sake, Pete,' I cried, gazing from him to the poor bleeding body in the chair, 'tell me why you did it?'

'Hold your jaw!' said he, twisting his handkerchief round his cut finger, and looking, as he did so, with eyes that were more like a demon's than a man's. 'But stay, if

you want to know why I did it, I'll tell you.
I did it because the rope is round all our
necks, and if you move only as much as a
finger contrary to what I tell you, you'll hang
us and yourself into the bargain.'

Here the mysterious, One-eyed Doctor reeled
out into the verandah, and next moment I
heard him being violently sick over the rails.
By the time he returned, Pete had tied up
his hand, and was bending over the figure
in the chair.

'He's dead,' he said to the Doctor. Now,
we've got to find out what's best to be done
with him. Jim, you're in a tight place, and
must help us all you know.'

'For God's sake explain yourself, Pete!'
I cried, in an agony. 'How can I do anything if you don't. Why did you do it?'

'I'll tell you,' he answered, 'and in as few
words as possible, for there is no time to
waste. 'This individual is a Sydney detective
(here he pointed to the dead man). The horse
you rode in the race to-day is none other than
Gaybird, the winner of the Victorian Grand
National and the Sydney Steeplechase. The
Doctor there and I stole him from his box
at Randwick, three months ago, and brought
him out here by a means we understand. In-

formation was given to the police, and Jarman followed him. He got in tow with me. I recognised him the moment I set eyes on him, and invited him to dinner to - night. When you turned up the second time he must have imagined it was the local trooper whom he had ordered to meet him here, and decided to arrest us. He found out his mistake, and that is the result. Now you know how you stand. You must help us, for one moment's consideration will show you that you are implicated as deeply as we are. If this business is discovered, we shall all swing; if the horse racket is brought home, the three of us will get five years apiece, as sure as we're born : so don't you make any mistake about that!'

'But I am innocent,' I cried. 'I had nothing whatever to do with either the murder or the stealing of the horse.'

'Take that yarn to the police, and see what they will say to you. Look here!'

He crossed to the dead man again and fumbled in his coat pocket. Next moment he produced three blue slips of paper—one of which he opened and laid on the table before me. It was a warrant for my arrest.

'This is your doing, Pete,' I cried. 'Oh,

what a fool I was ever to have anything to do with you.'

I fell back against the wall sick and giddy. To this pass had all my folly brought me. Well might Sheilah have prophesied that my obstinacy would end in disaster.

'My God, what are we to do?' I cried, in an agony of terror as thought succeeded thought, each blacker and more hopeless than the last. 'If the man expected help from the township it may be here any minute. For Heaven's sake let us get that body out of the way before it comes.'

'You begin to talk like a man,' said Pete, rising from the chair in which he had seated himself. 'Let us get to business, and as quickly as possible.'

The Doctor got up from his chair and approached the murdered man.

'The first business must be to get rid of this,' he asked; 'but how?'

'We must bury him somewhere,' said Pete. 'Where do you think would be the best place?'

'Not near here, at any rate,' said the Doctor. 'Remember when he doesn't put in an appearance after a few days they'll be sure to overhaul this house and every inch of the grounds. No, it must be done at once, and miles away.'

'You're right as usual, Doctor,' said Pete. Then turning to me he continued, 'Look here, Jim—this falls to your share. I have schemed for it and worked it out, so don't you fail me. This morning I sent away a mob of five hundred fat cattle *via* Bourke to Sydney. Yates is in charge for the reason that I could get nobody else. At the present moment they'll probably be camped somewhere near the Rocky Waterhole. You must set off after them as hard as you can go, and take over the command. Do you see? You can take my bay horse, Archer, for your own riding, a pack horse, and for a part of the way, The Unknown, with this strapped on his back and properly hidden. You'll go across country as far as the Blackfellow's Well at the dip in the Ranges; once there, you'll bury him up among the rocks, conceal the place as craftily as you can, and drop the spade into the well. After that you'll go on to Judson's Boundary fence, where you'll be met by a man on a grey horse. You'll hand The Unknown over to him, and then hurry on as fast as you can travel to catch up the cattle. Having taken over the command, you'll see them on to Bourke, deliver them to Phillips, the agent, and then come back here as if nothing had happened.'

'But why can't you take the body, Pete? Why should you push it on to me?'

'Because, if I left here to-night, it would give the whole thing away. They will never suspect you. The Doctor and I must remain to answer inquiries.'

'But supposing the police visit the house to-night and search the stable, how will you account for the absence of the horse?'

'I sha'n't try to account for it at all. I've got a horse in the box now as like him as two peas. They can collar him if they want to, but there'll be one vital difference, I'll defy them to win a Grand National with him, let them be as clever as they will. But now let's get on with our work, it's close on twelve o'clock, and we haven't a moment to lose.'

Between them, Pete and the Doctor carried the body of the murdered detective out of the room, and I was left alone to think over my position. But it did not need much thought to see what sort of a fix I was in. Supposing I went down to the township and gave evidence, I should hang Pete and do myself little good, for who in their sober senses, seeing that I had ridden the horse at the races that day, had backed him to win me a large stake, and was known to have spent the evening at Pete's house, besides having been hand and glove with him for weeks past, would believe me innocent? Not one! No, everything was against me, and the only chance for me now was to fall in with their plans and to save my own neck by assisting them to carry them out to the best of my ability — at any rate, the fright I had experienced had made me as sober as a judge.

In about ten minutes Pete returned to the room.

'Now, Jim,' he said, 'everything is ready. Here's a note to Yates telling him I've sent you to take charge, and another to Phillips at Bourke. If you're going to do what we want you'd better be off. Anything to say first?'

'Only that I hope you see what I'm doing for your sake, Pete,' I answered. 'You know I'm as innocent as a babe unborn, and you're making me appear guilty. I'm fool enough to let you do it. But all the same I don't know that it's altogether square on your part.'

'Don't you, Jim? Then, by Jove! you sha'n't do it. I like you too well to let you run the risk of saving me against your will. Ride away down to the police station as hard as you can go, if you like, and tell them everything. Only don't upbraid me when I'm trying to save your neck as well as my own.'

Though I knew I was an arrant fool to do it, when he spoke like that I couldn't desert him. So I followed him out of the room into the yard like the coward I was.

Directly I got there I came to a sudden stop.

'This won't do at all,' I said. 'Look here, I'm dressed for the races and not for over-landing.'

And so I was. Whatever happened, I knew I must change my things.

'Take the horses down to the Creek Bend,' I said. 'I'll run home as fast as I can—change my duds, get my whip, and meet you there.'

He nodded, and off I set as hard as I could go—forded the creek, and in less than a quarter of an hour was back once more at my old home. Not a light of any kind shone from it. Seeing this, I crept round to my own window. Then, lifting the sash as quietly as I possibly could, I crept in like a thief. Knowing exactly where to find the things I wanted, in less than ten minutes I had changed my

clothes, packed my valise, and let myself out
again. Then down the track I sped once
more, to find Pete waiting with the three
horses in the shadow of a gum.

'I've been counting the minutes since you
left,' he cried impatiently, as I buckled my
valise on to the pack-saddle. 'Now jump up
and be off. Keep away from the township,
and steer for the well as straight as you can go.
You ought to be at the camp before daybreak.'

As he spoke he led the horses out of the
shadow, and I was in the act of mounting
when he suddenly dragged them back into it
once more.

'Quiet for your life,' he whispered; 'here
are the troopers, coming up the path.'

Sure enough, on the other side, three
mounted troopers were riding up the track. A
heavy sweat rose on my forehead as I thought
what would happen if one of our horses were
to move or neigh and so draw their attention
to us. With the body in the pack-saddle, we
should be caught red-handed.

Morgan, our township officer, rode a little in
advance, the two other troopers behind him.
They were laughing and joking, little dreaming how close we stood to them. When they
had safely passed, Pete turned to me. 'Now,'

he whispered, 'as soon as they are out of hearing be off as hard as you can go. I shall slip through the wattles and be back at the house and smoking with the Doctor in the verandah before they can reach it.'

The troopers went on up the track, and, when they got on to the top of the hill, turned off sharp to the left. As they disappeared from view I took a horse on either side of me, not without a shudder, as I thought of The Unknown's burden, and set off through the scrub towards some slip rails at the top of Pete's selection, which I knew would bring me out a little to the northward of the township. By the time the troopers could have reached the house I was through the fence and making my way down the hill as fast as my beasts could travel. It was a beautiful starlight night now, without a cloud or a breath of wind. Within a quarter of an hour I had left the last house behind me, and was heading away towards the south-west, across the open plain that surrounded the township on its northern side. Then, plunging into the scrub again, I made for the Blackfellow's Well as straight as I could steer. Considering the hard race he had run that day and the additional weight he was now carrying, The

Unknown was wonderfully fresh, and the other two horses found it took them all their time to keep pace with him.

The silence of the scrub was mysterious in the extreme, 'possums scuttled across my track, a stray dingoe had a long stare at me from some rocks above a creek, while curlews whistled at me from every pool. I hardly dared look at the bundle strapped upon the thoroughbred's back, and yet I knew that when half my journey was done I should have to undertake a still more gruesome bit of business.

By two o'clock I was within sight of the well, as it was called. It was more like a deep pool than a well, however, and lay in the shadow of a high rock. It derived its name from a superstition that existed in the neighbourhood that on a certain night in every year the blacks came down and cleaned it out. It was one of the loneliest spots in the district, and as it lay in a barren region, remote from the principal stock and travelling route, it was not visited by the general public more than once or twice a year. A better place could not have been selected for burying the man Pete had killed.

On arrival at the rock I jumped off and

secured the horses to a tree—then taking the shovel from the old pack horse's back I set off, clambering up among the rocks, on the look-out for a likely spot where I might dig the grave. At last, having discovered a place that I thought suitable, I set to work. The ground was hard, and nearly half-an-hour had elapsed before I had dug a deep enough hole for my purpose. Then putting down my shovel I went back to the well. The horses stood just as I had left them, and as soon as I had assured myself that there was not a soul about to spy upon me, I unstrapped the body and took it in my arms. However long I may live I shall never be able to rid myself of the horror of that moment. Having taken my ghastly burden in my arms, I set off, staggering and clambering up the hillside again till I found the grave I had dug. Then, when I had laid the body in it, I began hastily to cover it with earth. The sweat rolled off my face in streams before I had finished, but not so much with the labour as by reason of the horrible nature of my work. I hardly dared look at what was before me, but worked away with stubborn persistence until the greater part of the earth I had taken out was replaced. Then using the handle of the shovel as a lever, I wedged a big rock, a step or two up the hill, over on one side, worked round, and undermined it on the other, and finally rolled it down upon the grave itself. When this was done it was completely hidden from the most prying gaze, and I knew that every day would hide it better. Then giving a hasty glance round me to see that no one was about, and that I had left nothing behind me to furnish a clue, I picked up the shovel and set off, as hard as I could go, down the hill towards the horses. Arriving at the well, I threw the shovel into the pool and watched it disappear from view—then, untying my animals, I mounted, and, with a somewhat lightened heart, resumed my journey. The horses were cold with standing so long, and we soon made up for lost time, arriving at Judson's Boundary fence shortly before half-past two. One thing struck me as peculiar, and that was how Pete could have communicated with the man, but surely enough at the corner of the fence was an individual seated on a grey horse and evidently waiting for me.

'Good evening,' he said, in a gruff voice, as I rode up. 'A nice night for travelling—ain't it?'

'A very nice night,' I answered, looking him carefully over, 'and pray who are you waiting for?'

'For a messenger from Whispering Pete,' he answered. 'Is this the horse?'

I informed him that it was, and gave him the reins of The Unknown. He looked at him pretty closely, and then wheeled him round.

'Good night,' he said, 'and good luck to you. I've got a hundred miles to do before sundown.'

'Good night,' I cried in return, and then changing my course, set off across country for the place where I knew I should find the cattle. The sun was in the act of rising from the night fog when I made them out and rode up to the camp. The fire burnt brightly, and the cook was bustling about getting breakfast. Seeing me, Yates, who was not at all a bad sort of fellow, sat up in his blankets and stared, as well he might.

'Well, bless my soul, and how on earth did you get here?' he cried, 'and now you're here, what do you want? Anything wrong?'

'No, of course not; what on earth should make you think so?' I replied. 'Only I happened to be going to Bourke on business, so Pete asked me to come on and take charge. 'Here's a letter from him to you.'

I took Pete's note out of my pocket and handed it to him. Having torn it open, he read it through slowly. When he had done so he said, 'Well, I'm precious glad. It was against my will that I came at all; now I'm free, and all the responsibility, and in this dry season there's plenty of that, rests upon your shoulders and not on mine. I don't envy you!'

'I must take my chance,' I said. 'Now, supposing we have breakfast, and afterwards get on the move.'

Yates stared in surprise, for I must have looked more dead than alive after my long night ride, and all the excitement I had passed through.

'You don't mean to say you intend going on before you've had a rest,' he cried. 'Why, man, you're a death's head already. No, let's wait a bit and have a sleep; the cattle are on good feed and water, and, if all's true that I hear, they won't get any more like it on the other side of the border.'

'I don't want a rest,' I said, 'and if I do I can take it in the saddle as we go along. Tell one of the blackboys to run up the horses, will you? and then we'll have breakfast and start.'

'As you please, of course,' he said, but it was evident that he regarded my proposal in the light of madness. He was not very fond of work, was Mr Yates, and never had been since I had first known him, which was a matter of well nigh fifteen years.

'In less than half-an-hour breakfast was ready, and, as soon as it was eaten, we mustered the cattle and got under way. It was not a very big mob, but the animals were all valuable, and in the pink of condition.

To those who have never seen a mob of cattle on the march, the picture they present would be a novel and exciting one. Imagine marching on ahead, day after day, as proud as a drum-major, some old bull, the leader of the mob; behind him are some hundreds of cattle; on either flank vigilant stockmen ride, ever on the look-out for stragglers; the drover in command and the rest of the party follow as whippers-in, while the cart containing the blankets, camp and cooking utensils, driven by the cook, travels on some miles ahead. The latter individual chooses the night's camp, prepares it, and has the evening meal cooked and ready by the time the mob puts in

an appearance.   After nightfall, a perpetual
two hours' watch is kept by mounted men,
while emergency horses are fastened near the
camp to be ready in the event of a stampede
or other trouble occurring.

Our journey, in this instance, was an un-
eventful one, lasting something like six weeks.
When we reached Bourke, and had handed
over our cattle to the agent for trucking to
Sydney, our mission was accomplished. As
soon, therefore, as I had obtained my receipt
from Mr Phillips, the agent to whom the mob
was consigned, I took the train to Sydney,
and once there hunted about for a medium-
sized class hotel where I could put up while
I remained in the metropolis. A big city
was a new experience to me, and you may
be sure I made the most of my opportunity of seeing it; at the same time, I
kept a watchful eye on the daily papers
for anything that transpired at Barranda during my absence. But from what I could
gather, nothing unusual seemed to have
happened in that sleepy hollow; so I was
gradually recovering my old peace of mind
when I received a shock that knocked my feeling of security about my ears again. I had
been to the theatre one night, I remember,

and was standing outside the door, after the fall of the curtain, thinking about getting back to my hotel, when who should come along the pavement but Finnan, the One-eyed Doctor, himself, dressed in evening clothes, and looking as contented and happy as you please. He seemed a bit surprised, not to say *nonplussed*, at seeing me, but shook hands with every appearance of heartiness. Then putting his arm through mine, he led me into a side street.

'You managed that bit of business splendidly,' he said, when we were sure there was no one near enough to overhear us. 'Pete was delighted at the way you did it.'

'Has anything turned up about it yet?' I asked anxiously.

'Nothing important,' be answered. 'The Government are wondering what can have become of Jarman, who is supposed to have gone north, but the people in the township have discovered somehow that Pete is suspected of having stolen Gaybird. Of course, they all implicate you in it; and if I were you I should keep out of their way till the fuss blows over.'

This was unpleasant hearing with a vengeance, but I was not going to let him see that I thought it, so I said,—

'Where is Pete now?'

'Goodness only knows. He remained hanging about the township for a fortnight after you went away, just to allay suspicion, then he announced that he was off to buy cattle on the Diamintina. Since then he has not been heard of.'

'A nice kettle of fish he has let me in for,' I answered hotly. 'I can't say that I think he has acted at all like a man.'

'I don't know that I think he has acted altogether fairly towards you,' said the agreeable Doctor. 'However, what's done can't be undone; so I suppose we must make the best of it. Anything more to say? Nothing? Well, perhaps we'd better not be seen together for very long, so good night!'

I bade him good night, and having done so, walked slowly back to my hotel, wondering what was best to be done. To remain away from the township would look as if I were afraid of facing its inhabitants. And yet it was pretty dangerous work going back there. However, knowing my own innocence, I wasn't going to give them the right to call me guilty, so I determined to risk it, and accordingly next morning off

I set for Bourke *en route* for the Cargoo
again. In about a fortnight I had reached
the township.

Darkness had fallen when I rode up the
main street, and as I did not know quite
what to do with myself now that I had no
home to go to, I halted at the principal
hotel and installed myself there. A good
many men were in the bar when I entered,
and from the way one and all looked at me,
I could see that they were aware of the
rumours that were afloat concerning me.
However, nobody said anything on the subject, so I called for a glass of whiskey and,
having drunk it, went into the dining-room,
where about a dozen people were seated at
the table. I took my place alongside a man
I had known ever since we were kiddies
together, and more for the sake of making
myself agreeable than anything else, said
'good evening' to him. He replied civilly
enough, but I could see that he did not
care to be friendly, and, when he made an
excuse and went round and sat on the other
side of the table, I saw significant glances
flash round the board. 'All right,' I
thought to myself, 'I'll say nothing just now,
but the first man who drops a hint about that

horse or my connection with the race, I'll go for tooth and nail, if it costs me my life.' But never a hint *was* dropped, and when the meal was over I went out into the verandah to rage alone. I was in an unenviable position, and the worst part of it all was, I had nothing to thank for it but my own consummate obstinacy and stupidity.

About nine o'clock I filled my pipe afresh and set off for a stroll down the street, keeping my eyes open to see if any of my old friends would take notice of me. But no one did till I had almost left the township. Then an elderly man, by name Bolton, who kept one of the principal stores in Main Street, and had always been a special crony of mine, crossed the road and came towards me.

'Jim Heggarstone,' said he, when he got on to the footpath alongside me, 'I want to have a few words with you, if you don't mind.'

'I'm your man!' I answered. 'Shall we sit on the rail here, or would you rather walk along a bit?'

'No, let us sit here,' he replied, and as he spoke, mounted the fence; 'we're not likely to be interrupted, and I don't know that it would matter particularly if we were. Look here, Jim, I've always been your friend, and I am now. But certain things have been said about you of late in the township that I tell you frankly are not to your credit. What I want is authority to deny them on your behalf.'

'You must first tell me what they are,' I answered; 'you can't expect a chap to go about explaining his actions every time a township like this takes it into its head to invent a bit of tittle-tattle against him. What have they to say against me? Out with it.'

'Well, in the first place, they say that Whispering Pete on the hill up yonder knew that the horse he raced as The Unknown was Gaybird, the winner of the Victorian Grand National and the Sydney Steeple-chase. Do you think that's true?'

'How can I say? He may or may not have known it. But I don't see that it has anything to do with me if he did?'

'No! Perhaps not! But you will when I tell you that it's also said that you were aware of it too, and that you laid your plans accordingly.'

'Whoever says that tells a deliberate false-hood,' I cried angrily. 'I did not know it. If I had I would rather have died than have ridden him.'

'I know that, Jim,' he answered, and so I have always said. Now, if you will let me, I'll call the next man who says so a liar to his face, on your behalf.'

'So you shall, and I'll ram it down his throat with my fist afterwards. This has been a bad business for me, Bolton. In the first place, I have been kicked out of doors by my father for riding that race, and now my character is being taken away in this shabby fashion for a thing I'm quite innocent of.'

'You ought never to have got in tow with Whispering Pete, Jim.'

'Nobody knows that better than I do!' I cried bitterly. 'But it's too late to alter it now.'

'Well, good night. And keep your heart up. Things will come right yet. And remember, Jim, I'm your friend through all.'

We shook hands, and having done so, the kind-hearted fellow went his way down the street while I strolled on as far as the McLeods' homestead. There was a light shining from the sitting-room window, and

Sheilah McLeod

I could hear the music of a piano. Then Sheilah's pretty voice came out to me singing a song, of which I am very fond. The words are Kingsley's, I believe, and the last verse seemed so appropriate to my case, that it brought a lump into my throat that almost choked me. It ran as follows :—

> When all the world is old, lad,
> And all the trees are brown,
> And all the sport is stale, lad,
> And all the wheels run down,
> Creep home, and take your place there,
> The spent and maimed among ;
> God grant you find one face there
> You loved when all was young.

CHAPTER VI

COLIN McLEOD

NEXT morning as soon as I had finished my breakfast I put on my hat and went down to McLeod's selection, resolved to find out once and for all in what sort of light I stood with Sheilah. In my own inmost heart I knew that I deserved to be shown the door on presenting myself, but somehow I had a sort of conviction that my fate would not be quite as hard as that. Reaching the gate, I let myself in, and walked down the path, under the little avenue of pepper-trees, that entwined overhead, to the house. Everything was just as I had left it, but, oh, how different were my own feelings!

I found old McLeod on his knees in the verandah fastening up some creepers that had fallen out of place. When he saw me he rose and without a second thought came forward and shook me warmly by the hand.

'Welcome home, James, my lad,' said he, looking me full and square in the face, 'I'm glad ye've come back to us, and so will Sheilah be, ye may depend. Ye've been a long time away.'

This kindly reception was more than I had bargained for, and like the big baby I was I felt the hot tears rise and flood my eyes. There was that in my heart then which would have made me lay down my life for old McLeod if need have been. That was always the way with me, I could be brought to do anything by kindness, when force could not make me budge an inch. For the self-same reason old Betty at home had always been able to manage me—my father never.

'Mr McLeod,' said I, as I returned the pressure of the hand he held out to me, a hand that was as knotted and gnarled as any ti-tree in the scrub, 'after all that has happened this is a generous way for you to receive me. Do you know that only one soul in the township up yonder has spoken to me since my return.'

'I'm sorry to hear that, James,' said he, seating himself in a chair near by, and mopping his forehead with his red pocket-handkerchief. 'No young man can afford to lose his friends in that extravagant fashion.'

'Do you know the charge they bring against me?'

'I have heard it,' he answered, looking straight at me. 'But I think it only right to ye to say that I do not believe it all the same.'

'It is not true, so help me, God,' I burst out impetuously. 'If I had dreamt that the horse had been stolen I would no more have ridden him in that race than I would have shot him. I hope you know me well enough to believe that, Mr McLeod.'

'I think I do,' he answered; 'at any rate, this has been a lesson that should last you all your life.'

'It has,' I answered bitterly; 'but all the same I don't think I have been at all fairly treated over it. Whispering Pete was generous to me, and when he asked me to do him the favour of riding his horse I could not refuse. Then I was told by my father that he would turn me out of doors if I did not obey him. But having given my promise to Pete, how could I be expected to break it again?'

'James, James,' the old man said, when I had finished, 'the devil had ye in a tight place just then, and ye ought to thank God right down on your bended knees that He has permitted ye to come out of it as well as ye have. I shall say a word for ye next Sunday, and if ye'll mind what's right ye'll be there to hear it.'

'That I will,' I answered, completely carried away by the good old man's earnestness. 'Mr McLeod, you've treated me as I did not expect I should be treated, and I'll never forget it as long as I live. Now, may I see Sheilah?'

'And why not, laddie? Of course ye may, and right glad the lassie will be to have ye back again, I'll warrant. She's out with her chickens just now, I fancy, for I saw her going down the path with her egg basket on her arm but a wee bit since. Go and find her, and hear for yourself what she has to say to ye.'

I went round the verandah, passed Sheilah's own window, with its little cluster of pot plants on the sill, and then down the path towards the fowl-yard. True enough, there she was, dressed all in white, with her pretty face looking out from the large blue sun-bonnet she always wore on summer mornings. At first she did not see me, so I stood still watching her. One thing I can always assert, and that is that I have seen many pretty girls in my time, but never one to equal Sheilah. There was a softness and natural grace about her that was beyond the power of other girls to imitate; a grace which could never have been taught in any school or dancing academy. And as I watched my heart rose in love to her, then I suppose I must have made some noise among the bushes, for she suddenly turned round and stood face to face with me. As she saw me a glad smile leapt into her face, and she ran towards me with hands outstretched in welcome.

'Jim, dear old Jim,' she cried, 'I knew you would come back to us before long. Oh, I have missed you so dreadfully! Remember, you have been away nearly two months.'

'Don't, Sheilah!' I cried, 'don't speak so kindly to me. Scold me a little or I shall make a fool of myself, I know.'

'Scold you!' she cried, with her little hands in mine. 'Scold you, old Jim, when you're only just come back to us. Oh no, no! This is, indeed, a happy day. Have you seen my father? He was talking of you only this morning.'

'I left him to come to you. His welcome was as warm as yours. Oh, Sheilah, I feel that I have been such a brute to you. And it hurts me the more because I know you will so freely forgive me.'

'Hush, we will not talk of that. All that part of your life is done with and put away. It was a miserable time for all of us, but thank goodness it's over.'

Just at that moment a young man appeared from the fowl-house and came towards us with some eggs in his hand.

'I can find no more,' he said to Sheilah. Then he looked at me with a searching glance, and did not seem altogether pleased.

'Jim,' said Sheilah, noticing my surprise, 'this is my cousin, Colin McLeod, who has come up to be our new trooper in Barranda. He has only been eighteen months in the Colonies, and was sent out from Brisbane last week. Colin, this is my old playfellow of whom you have so often heard me speak, Jim Heggarstone.'

We nodded to each other, and when I saw that he was going to make the eggs he held an excuse for not shaking hands with me, I put my own in my pockets, and stared hard at him. He was a fine, well-set-up young fellow of about my own age, with blue eyes and peculiar sandy-coloured hair.

'Now,' said Sheilah, who must have noticed that it was not all plain sailing with us, 'suppose we go inside and see what my father is doing. He intended to brand some colts this morning, and if he does I expect you'd like to help him in the yard, Jim?'

'Of course I should,' I answered readily enough. 'I'm pining to get to work again.'

'You have not been doing much work lately, then,' says Mr Colin, with a shadow of a sneer.

'I've just returned from taking a mob of cattle down to Bourke,' I answered.

'Ah!' was his sole reply, and then we went into the house.

Half-an-hour later I was with old McLeod in the yards, had the fire for heating the branding-irons lighted, and was running the green hide lasso through my hands to see that it was supple and ready for use. I don't want to boast, seeing that, all things considered, I'd far better be holding my tongue, but lasso-ing was a thing I could challenge any man in the country at. However, I was not so successful on this occasion. Whether it was Colin McLeod sitting on the rails watching me, or whether it was that I was out of practice, I cannot say; I only know that time after time I missed, and on each occasion, as the noose fell to the ground, I saw the sneer spread out on Colin's face, and once I could have sworn I heard him chuckle. But I managed to keep my temper under control. Then my old skill suddenly returned, and after a while I could not miss a beast. But here I must do Colin justice. For a new chum he was as good a man in the yard as ever I've met, being quiet and gentle with the beasts, and, what is still more to the point, always ready to do what he was told. He only wanted practice to make a really good hand. I found occasion to tell him so when the work was finished, and I could have bitten my tongue out with vexation when he replied with his long Scotch drawl, still with the same diabolical sneer on his face,—

'Ye see, I've not had so much experience with horses as ye've had, Mr Heggarstone.'

It was plain to what he referred, and it took me all my time, I can assure you, to prevent my tongue from replying something sharp. However, I had no desire to celebrate my return to the selection by thrashing the owner's nephew, so I did manage to control myself, and side by side we returned to the house. At first, seeing how things stood, I was for going back to the township for lunch, but of this neither Sheilah nor her father would hear. So I was forced to stay where I was and endure the other man's treatment as best I could. One thing was very plain, and that was that Colin was madly in love with Sheilah. He could hardly take his eyes off her, almost trembled when he addressed her, lost no opportunity of doing her little services, and glared madly at me whenever I spoke to her or attempted to do anything for her. It was a queer sight, and one that was not calculated to fill me with pleasure, you may be sure. At last, after the mid-day meal was over, his conduct became so outrageous that I made the first excuse that suggested itself and said good-bye, promising to come down again next day. As I shook hands with her, Sheilah looked at me with rather a wistful expression on her face, I thought; while even old McLeod seemed to wonder that my first visit should terminate so abruptly.

To tell the truth, however, I could not have bottled up my feelings another minute; so rather than make an exhibition of myself I preferred to go away.

Back I went to the hotel, my whole being raging against the man. In the face of this rivalry I learned what Sheilah really was to me, and for the first time I understood how I should feel if any man were to win her from me.

Next day, according to promise, I went down to the selection again, to find Sheilah sitting in the verandah. She was alone and received me very sweetly. I sat beside her talking of old days, and firmly resolved not to let her imagine that I had been in any way put out by her cousin's curious behaviour on the preceding day.

'We must celebrate your return in some way, Jim,' she said after a little while. 'It is a lovely morning, so what do you say to a ride?'

'The very thing!' I answered, only too thankful to do anything that would take me away from the house, and prevent my seeing the irate Colin again.

With that we went out to the back, and borrowing the milkboy's pony, I ran up two horses from the paddock for our use. After

I had rubbed them down a bit I saddled them, and by the time I had done this Sheilah was dressed and ready. With a thrill running through me such as I had never known before, I swung her up into the saddle, and then mounted my own beast; after that, when the boy had let down the slip rails, away we went across the plains towards the hills. It was as lovely a morning as any man could wish to be out in. The soft breeze rustled among the trees and high grass, the clouds chased each other across the blue vault of heaven, the air was musical with birds, and now and again we would put up a kangaroo and send him hopping away from us as if his very life depended upon it. Sheilah was in the best of spirits and looked incomparably sweet and graceful. Just swaying to the motion of her horse as he covered the ground in a gentle canter, her body well balanced and her head thrown back, the wind nodding the feather in her pretty hat, and just a suspicion of a neat little boot showing beneath her habit, she made a picture pretty enough for a king. And now that Colin McLeod had come to make me understand how much I really loved her, I was induced to notice her beauties even more closely than before.

For nearly an hour we rode on, all the past forgotten, living only in the keen enjoyment of the present. Then, like a flash, the memory of my ride to the Blackfellow's Well—part of the very route we were now pursuing—rose before me. I saw again the dark night, the flashing tree trunks, the horses galloping on either side of me, and that horrible burden swaying on The Unknown's back. Then I saw the Blackfellow's Well, pictured myself digging that lonely grave among the rocks, and seemed again to hear the curlews crying from the pool below. I suppose something of the horror of the memory must have been reflected on my face, for Sheilah looked at me and then said,—

'Jim, what is the matter? You're as pale as death.'

'Nothing,' I answered hoarsely. 'A twinge of an old pain, that is all.'

'It must have been a bad one,' she answered quietly. 'Your face looked really ghastly.'

'It has passed,' I cried, giving myself a vigorous shake. 'I don't know what brought it on. However, we'll have no more dismal thoughts to-day, Sheilah, by your leave.'

'That's right,' she answered. 'I do not like to see such an expression upon your

face.   Now let's turn round and go back by
the Pelican Waterhole.   See here's a nice
piece of turf, we can give our horses a gallop.'

The words were hardly out of her mouth
before she had shaken up her horse and we
were off like the wind.   Good as my animal
was, Sheilah's was better, and, when we
reached the fringe of timber on the opposite
side of the little plain, she was leading by a
good five lengths.   Then, seeing that the
ground did not look very safe ahead, I was
about to call to her to pull up, when her
horse crossed his legs, and went down with
a crash, throwing Sheilah, and rolling completely over her.

For a second my heart seemed to stand
still, then to the ground I sprang and ran
swiftly to her side.   Her horse by this time
had risen, and was shaking himself, but Sheilah
lay just as she had fallen, horribly white and
still.

'Sheilah!' I cried, as I knelt by her side,
'for pity's sake speak to me!'

But not a word came from her pallid lips,
and seeing this I picked up my heels and ran
to the creek for water.   Filling my cabbage-
tree hat I hurried back to her, but by the time
I reached her she was conscious once more.

'Jim,' she said, with a fine show of bravery, 'this is a very bad business. I'm dreadfully afraid I've broken my leg. What am I to do? I can't get up.'

'Oh, Sheilah, you don't mean that!' I cried in agony. 'It's all my fault, I should not have brought you for this ride.'

'Don't be silly, Jim,' she answered stoutly. 'It was not your fault at all. But what am I to do? We are at least four miles from home?'

I considered for a moment before I answered.

'If you can't move, the best thing for me to do would be to make you as comfortable as possible here, and then ride off as fast as I can go for the tray buggy and a mattress. We could bring you in in that way better than any other.'

'That's it, Jim. Now go as fast as you can. My poor father will be in a terrible state when he hears the news.'

'First let me make you as comfortable as possible,' I replied. 'I think it would be better for you to lie just where you are.'

Taking off my coat, I rolled it into a pad. Next I caught her horse and removed her saddle. This I placed flaps upward, beneath her head, with my coat upon it, and so made a fairy comfortable pillow.

'Do you feel easier now?' I asked, looking down at her.

'Much easier,' she answered; 'but don't be any longer than you can help, Jim.'

'Not a second,' I replied, and ran towards my own horse and climbed into the saddle. Then with a last call of encouragement I set off, and within half-an-hour was at the stable slip panels. Then without waiting to let them down I sprang off and ran into the house. Old Mrs Beazley, the cook, was standing at her kitchen door.

'Where is Mr McLeod?' I asked, almost trembling with excitement.

'Gone up to the township,' she answered. 'What is the matter? Has anything happened?'

'Miss Sheilah has met with an accident out by Pelican Creek,' I answered. 'She thinks she has broken her leg. You had better send for the doctor and her father at once. In the meantime, I'll take the buggy and a matress, if you will give me one, and go out and bring her in?'

At this moment Colin McLeod, with a face the colour of zinc, appeared from the house and stood staring at me.

'What's that you say?'

'Sheilah has broken her leg out yonder. I'm going with the buggy to bring her in. If you like you can come and help me lift her,' I answered, all my former animosity forgotten in this new and greater trouble.

'Come on,' he cried in a voice I hardly recognised. 'Are you going to stand talking all day?'

He ran into the yard as he spoke, and after giving a final instruction to Mrs Beazley, I followed, to find him leading a horse from the stable. Without a word I went to the coach-house and drew out McLeod's big tray buggy, took the harness from the peg and threw it down by the horse's nose, then back into the house again for the mattress Mrs Beazley was stripping off a bed for me. This I placed on the tray, and by the time I had done so the horse was harnessed and ready for putting in. Colin held up the shafts while I backed him to his place. By the time this was done the slip rails were down and I drove through. Then Colin sprang up beside me, and off we went across the plain towards the place where I had left Sheilah.

When we reached it we found her lying exactly as I had left her. Colin jumped down, ran to her side, and said something in a low voice that I did not catch. Without losing a second, I lifted the seat from its place and lowered it overboard; then I, too, jumped down and went towards the sufferer.

'How can we lift you, do you think, with the least likelihood of hurting you?' I asked.

'I don't know,' she answered. 'I think you had better put the mattress down here beside me, and then lift me on to it.'

I saw the wisdom of this idea, and forthwith dragged the mattress out and laid it on the ground by her side. Then, with all the tenderness of which we were capable, Colin and I lifted her and placed her on it. She paled a little while we were doing it, but did not let a sound escape her. After that I brought the buggy as close as possible, helped Colin to lift the mattress on to the tray, and then climbed aboard and placed her in such a position that her head lay against the splashboard. Having done this, I signed to Colin to hand me the saddle and my coat, with which I once more constructed a pillow for her. The seat was then refixed without touching her, and her own horse having been fastened on behind, I chose the straightest and least rutty track, and set off slowly for the homestead. It took us nearly an hour to reach it, and when we did old McLeod met us at the slip rails. He looked very nervous, but bore up bravely for Sheilah's sake.

Pulling the buggy up at the kitchen door, we withdrew the seat again, removed the pillows, and then lifted our precious burden down. Just as we did so the doctor rode up to the door, and, having tied his horse to the fence, gave us a hand to carry Sheilah to her room. Then leaving her to his care, with Mrs Beazley to assist him, we went into the verandah, where Mr McLeod asked me to tell him how it had happened.

I gave him a full description of it, but though it appeared to satisfy him it was more than it did for Colin, who listened with the same expression on his face that was always there when I was present. How it was that I had aroused such antagonistic feelings in him I could not imagine. Whether he would have been the same with any other rival I could not tell, but that he hated me with all the strength of his powerful nature was plain to the least observant. After I had finished my narrative, and had discovered that I could do no more good by remaining, I rose to say good-bye.

'Good-bye, James, my lad,' said the old man,

giving me his hand. 'I know that what has happened has given you as much pain as it has me. But, remember, you must not reproach yourself. It was in no way your fault. And are you going too, Colin, my lad?'

'I'm on duty this afternoon,' Colin said, putting on his hat, 'and I must get back and prepare for it. Good-bye, uncle!'

'Good-bye, my lad.'

Old McLeod retired into the house, and we went up the garden path together. When we got into the road outside, Colin McLeod turned to me and said, 'Have you any objection to my walking a little way with you? I've got something I want to say to you.'

'Come along, then,' I answered, 'and say it for mercy's sake. I'm sick of all these black looks and sarcastic speeches. What is it? Out with it!'

'It's this,' he said. 'First and foremost, I'll have no more of you down yonder.' He nodded his head in the direction of his uncle's house.

'Indeed! and, pray, what right have you to say you will, or you won't?'

'If you don't know, I'll tell you,' he answered; 'but I think you do!'

'I don't,' I answered, stopping and facing him, 'and I'll be glad if you will tell me.'

'Well, in the first place, I won't have you there because of that business with the man they call Whispering Pete, and, in the second, because, in my official capacity, I know more about you than my uncle and cousin do—and I tell you I won't let you mix with them.'

'Colin McLeod,' I said, looking him straight in the face, and speaking very slowly, 'you're either a plucky man or a most extraordinary fool. Remember this once and for all—neither you nor the whole police force of Australia know anything that would keep me away from my old friends the McLeods. And if you say you do, well, I tell you you're a liar to your face. So there now!'

'Fair and softly,' he said in reply. 'Listen to what I have to say before you talk so big. I tell you we know a good deal more than you think we do, and when we lay our hands on Whispering Pete we shall know still more. In the meantime, I'm not going to trade on my official knowledge against you. I'll meet you as man to man, and chance the consequences. I tell you that I love my cousin to desperation, and I'm not going to have a man like you hanging round her. Keep away from her, and I'll do no more than my duty demands. Continue to visit them, and, I warn you, you'll have to take the consequences.'

'And what are the consequences, pray?' I said, wishing he would come to the point.

'That you'll have to deal with me,' he answered, as if he were threatening me with death.

'That's rather big talking on your part, isn't it?' I asked. 'I don't know that I'm altogether afraid of dealing with you.'

'I'm glad to hear you say that! Now, will you fight me for her?'

He stopped in his walk and, turning round, clutched me by the arm.

'No, I will not,' I replied firmly, at the same time feeling that I would have given anything in the world to have been able to answer 'Yes.'

'I thought not,' he continued, with a sigh. 'You're a coward, and I knew it.'

'Steady! steady!' I said. 'One more remark like that and you'll get into trouble.'

'Then let me see if this will help you,' he cried, and at the same time he lifted his arm and hit me a hard blow across the mouth with the back of his left hand. I was about to strike back, when I suddenly changed my mind.

'You have raised your hand to me,' I said quietly. 'And a blow dealt in anger I'll take from no man on God's earth, much less you, Colin McLeod. I refused to fight you just now—for the simple reason that you are Sheilah's kith and kin. But since you've struck me, I'd do it if you were her own blood brother. One thing first, however. Be so good as to do me the justice to remember that you yourself have forced the quarrel on me.'

'I will remember,' he said sullenly. 'And where is it to be?'

'Down in the bit of scrub by the Big Gum at the creek bend,' I answered. 'We're not likely to be disturbed there.'

'At eight to-night. I am on patrol duty and can't get away before.'

I nodded, and then we separated; he went up the hill to the police station, while I continued my walk towards the township. As I went I thought over my position; here was another pretty fix I had got myself into. My old luck had certainly deserted me, for what would Sheilah say, if by any chance she should come to hear of it. When all was said and done, however, was it my fault? I didn't want to fight the man, I would far rather not have done so, but since he had struck the first blow I could not very well get out of it. Any man who knows me will tell you that I haven't the reputation of being a coward. Ruminating in this fashion I went on up the street to my hotel, and arrived there as the lodgers were sitting down to lunch. While I was eating, a curious notion seized me. What if I went up to the old home and interviewed my father? I had quite lived down my animosity, and if he proved willing to forgive I was quite ready to do the same.

As soon, therefore, as I rose from the table I went to my room, tidied myself up a bit, and set off. It seemed an eternity since I had forded the creek and trod that familiar path. I recalled with a shudder that horrible night when I had sneaked home to change my things prior to going off to bury Jarman. It was like a part of another life to look back on now—a nightmare, the remembrance of which always seized me in my happiest moments—like the skeleton at the Egyptian feast. And all the time I had to remember that the horrible secret lay hidden under those rocks only waiting for some chance passer-by to discover it.

At last I reached the verandah and paused upon the threshold like a stranger, not knowing quite what to do. My doubts, however, were soon set at rest by the appearance of my father in the passage. A great change had come over him. He looked years older, and was evidently a much feebler man than when I had left him last. So different was he that the shock almost unnerved me. But I soon saw that his disposition had not changed very much.

'Good morning,' he said, just as if he were greeting a total stranger. 'Pray what can I do for you?'

'Father, I have come up to see if I can't induce you to forgive me, and let us patch this quarrel up!'

'I beg your pardon,' he answered slowly, but still with the same exquisite politeness; 'I don't know that I understand you. Did I understand you to address me by the title of father?'

'I am your son!'

He seated himself in one of the verandah chairs, and I noticed that his hand trembled on the arm as he laid it there.

'I have forgotten that I ever had a son,' he said, after a moment's pause, 'and I have no desire to be reminded of the disagreeable fact.'

'Then you will not forgive me,' I cried bitterly, amazed at his obstinacy.

'My son was a horse coper and a black-guard,' he continued, 'and even if I were

to admit him to my house I should certainly
not forgive him!'

'Thank you,' I said, moving towards the
steps to go away again. 'You wronged me
before—and now you do so again. I will
trouble you no more.'

'One moment before you go,' he cried,
tapping on the floor with his stick. 'You
have not come up here to work upon my
feelings without having some object in view,
I suppose. I hear you are living in the
township at the principal hotel, doing nothing
for your living. Your presence here means,
I presume, that you want money. If that
is so, I will give you five hundred pounds
to enable you to start afresh in the world,
provided you leave this place within twenty-
four hours, and do not let me ever see you
or hear of you again.'

'And you refuse me your forgiveness for
the wrong you have done me?'

'I am not aware that I have done you
any wrong,' he answered. 'I only believe
what everybody in the township down yonder
knows to be a fact. To-morrow morning
you shall have that money if you wish it.
After that I will not give you a halfpenny
to save you from starving.'

Then, as if to justify himself, he continued, 'I do it on principle.'

'Very good—then, on principle, I refuse
to receive even a penny from you.'

He looked at me in surprise.

'You won't take the five hundred pounds?'

'Not one halfpenny,' I answered; 'I would
not if I were dying. Good day.'

'You are very foolish. But you will
change your mind in a few hours; so may
I. Good day.'

Without more ado I left him and strode
angrily back to the township. Surely no
man ever had a more pig-headed, unnatural
father?

That evening, a few minutes before eight
o'clock, I left the hotel and strode off down
the path by the creek to the place where
I had arranged to meet Colin. Bitterly as
I hated him, and angry as I was over the
blow he had dealt me, I was not at all
reconciled to the notion of fighting him.
My position was already sufficiently pre-
carious without my endeavouring to make
it more so.

The moon was up, and it was a glorious
night. In the little open space where I sat
down to wait, it was almost as bright as

day. In a gum to the back of me a mopoke was hooting dolefully, and to my right, among the bracken, the river ran sluggishly along, the moonlight touching it like silver. It was the beginning of summer, and there was still sufficient water coming down from the hills to make a decent stream.

Almost punctually at eight o'clock Colin put in an appearance, and came across the open towards me.

'I was half afraid I might keep you waiting,' he said, as he took off his coat and threw it on the ground.

'You're punctual, I think,' I answered, rising. 'But look here, McLeod, I'm not going to fight you after all. I can't do it!'

'Turning cocktail again, are you?' he said coldly. 'Do you want me to find your courage for you in the same fashion as this morning?'

'Don't push me too far,' I said, 'or God alone knows what I may not do. I'm a bad man to cross, as you may have heard.'

'Your reputation is only too well known to me,' he answered. 'Are you going to stand up or not?'

'Since you wish it so much,' I said wearily, seeing that further argument was useless.

'I thought you would hear reason,' he said, and took up his position.

We faced each other, and he led off with a blow that caught me on the chin. That roused my blood, and there and then I let him have it. He was not a bad boxer, and by no means deficient in courage, but he was like a baby in my hands. I can say that safely without fear of bragging. Three times in succession I sent him down to measure his length upon the ground. And each time he got up and faced me again. At last I could stand it no longer.

'That's enough,' I cried. 'Good God, man, you don't know what you're doing! If I go on I shall murder you.'

'We'll go on then till you do,' he said, getting up for the fourth time and preparing to renew the battle. But just as he did so a loud voice behind us called 'Stop!'

It was old McLeod.

'And pray what does this mean?' he cried, as he came between us. 'James Heggarstone, I am ashamed of ye. Colin, surely ye must have taken leave of your senses.'

Then Colin gave me another sample of his curious character.

'You must not blame Heggarstone,' says he. 'I assure you it was all my fault. I challenged him, and when he refused to fight I struck him.'

I could not let him take all the blame in this fashion, so I was just going to chip in when old McLeod stopped me by holding up his hand.

'I don't care whose fault it is. Ye are both to blame. I've seen it coming on day by day, and I can tell ye both it has distressed me beyond measure. I'll have no more of it, remember. Ye'll shake hands, lads, here now, and be good friends for the future, or ye'll both quarrel with me.'

'I've no objection at all,' I said, holding out my hand.

'Nor I,' says Colin, doing the same.

And then and there we shook hands, and that was the last of my enmity with Colin McLeod.

CHAPTER VII

NEXT morning, as soon after breakfast as was fit and proper, I set off to inquire after Sheilah. I found her looking very pale and jaded, poor girl; and no wonder, for the business of setting the broken limb had been a painful one.

'Sit down,' she said, pointing to a chair by her sofa. 'I want to have a good talk with you. Jim, I hear you were fighting with Colin last night.'

I hung my head and did not answer.

'What you two should have to fight about I'm sure I don't know,' she went on. 'But, remember, I'll have no more of it. If I thought you were to blame I should be very angry with you. But Colin has already been here and cleared you of everything. Poor Colin!'

'I'm sorry I ever laid my hand upon him,' I said. 'He's a better man than I am by a good deal.'

'I'm not so sure of that, Jim,' she said, holding out her little hand to me; 'but, remember, on no account are you two to be anything but the very best of friends for the future. And now we'll forget all about it. I want to talk to you about another matter.'

'What is that, Sheilah?'

'About yourself. What do you intend to do? You must not—and, indeed, you cannot—go on living here without employment. Have you thought of looking for anything?'

'I have. And what's more I have made inquiries all round, but for the life of me I can hear of nothing. I'm no good for anything but bush work, as you know, or I might apply for the billet there is vacant in the bank up yonder. No, Sheilah! I'm afraid I shall have to clear out and look for work elsewhere. There's a drover, Billy Green of Bourke, going up North as far as the Flinders River for a mob of fat cattle next week. He might take me on.'

'No! no! Jim, you're fit for something better than that,' she answered. 'Why not stay here and take a place for yourself. With your knowledge of cattle, backed up by patience and hard work, you might make a very good thing of it in time.'

'There's one serious drawback to that,

Sheilah, and that is the fact that I haven't got the money. If I had, I admit I might be able to do something in a small way. But as I haven't, well, you must see for yourself it's impossible.'

'It's not so impossible as you imagine, old friend,' said Sheilah, with a smile.

'What do you mean?' I asked, surprised at the confident way in which she spoke. 'Has anyone told you of the money I refused to take from my father yesterday?'

'You refused to take money from your own father? Oh, Jim, that was foolish of you. How much did he offer you?'

'Five hundred pounds,' I answered. 'I almost wish now I had put my pride in my pocket and accepted it. It would have come in very handily, wouldn't it?'

'You must go up and see him directly you leave here,' she said with authority. 'Whatever you do, you must not let such an opportunity slip through your fingers. It was too foolish of you to decline his help.'

'I'm afraid I'm a very foolish fellow altogether, Sheilah,' I answered. 'But my father insulted me; he called me—well, never mind what he called me; at any rate, having done it, he said he would give me five hundred pounds, and not another halfpenny, if I were to come to him starving. I flared up in reply, and told him that I would not touch his money if I were dying, and came away in a huff.'

'Well, you must go back and get it now, whatever happens. Why, with five hundred pounds you might lay the foundation of a splendid fortune. Now, pay attention to me, and tell me if there is any place about here you would like to take?'

'I should just think there is. Why, there's Merriman's selection on the other side of the creek; it's as good a little place as any in the district, and better than most. I've been coveting it for years, and if I had the money I would take it, stock it by degrees, and as time went on, and opportunity served, get possession of the land on either side of it. Yes! If I had that place, I do believe I could make it pay.'

'How much capital would you want to take it and stock it?'

I picked up a bit of paper from the table by where I sat, and, finding a pencil, set to work to figure it all out. Sheilah was quite excited, and offered suggestions and corrections as we proceeded, like the clever little business woman she always was. At last it was done.

'I reckon,' I said, looking up at her from the

paper in my hand, 'that if I had eight hundred pounds cash, and a balance in the bank of five hundred more, I could do it, and I'm certain I could make a success of it. But, then, what's the use of all this calculation. I haven't got the money, and, what's more, I'm certain my father won't go higher than the five hundred he mentioned, even if he lets me have that now.'

Sheilah was silent for nearly a minute, looking out of the window to where the tall sunflowers were nodding their heads in the scorching glare. A little dry wind rustled through the garden and flickered a handful of earth on to the well-swept boards of the verandah. Then she turned to me again and said rather nervously,—

'Jim, you have known me a long time have you not?'

'What a question, Sheilah,' I cried. 'Why, I've known you ever since the night of the great storm—when you were a little toddling blue-eyed baby. Of course, I've known you a long time.'

'Well, in that case, you mustn't be angry with an old friend for making a suggestion.'

'Angry with you, Sheilah! Not if I know it. What is it you wish to say?'

'That—well, that you let me lend you the money. No! No don't speak,' she cried, seeing that I was about to interpose. 'Let me say what I want to say first, and then you can talk as much as you please. Yes! I repeat, let me lend you the money, Jim. My father, as you know, has always put by so much a year for me, to do as I like with, ever since I was born. The sum now amounts to nearly fifteen hundred pounds. Well, I want to lend you a thousand pounds of it. And that, with the five hundred from your father, will give you fifteen hundred pounds to begin with, or two hundred more than you consider necessary. There, Jim, I have done; now what have you to say?'

'What can I say? How can I tell you how deeply I am touched by your generosity and goodness. Oh, Sheilah! what a true friend you have always been to me.'

'You accept my offer, then, Jim?' she cried, her beautiful eyes at the same time filling with tears.

'I cannot,' I answered. 'Deeply as I am touched by it, I cannot. It would not be right.'

'Oh, Jim, I never thought you would refuse. You will break my heart if you do. I have been thinking this out ever since you returned from Bourke, and always hoping that I should be able to persuade you to accept it. And now you refuse!'

She gave a deep sigh, and the big tears trembled in her eyes as if preparatory to flowing down her cheeks.

'Don't you see my position, Sheilah?' I said. 'Can't you understand that if I took your money, and invested in this enterprise, and it did not turn out a success, I might never have the means of repaying you. No! At any cost I feel that I ought not to take it.'

'Jim, you are giving me the greatest disappointment I have ever had in my life. Really you are.'

'Do you mean it?'

'I do.'

'Will it really make you happy if I accept?'

'Perfectly happy.'

'Then I will do so. And may God bless you for it. By giving me this chance you are saving me.'

'You will work hard then, won't you, Jim?'

'I will work my fingers to the bone, Sheilah.'

It was as much as I could do to speak, so

great was my emotion. My brain surged with words, but my mouth could not utter them. I took her hand and kissed it tenderly. A declaration of love trembled on my tongue, and wanted but one little word to make me pour it out.

'You must go and see your father this afternoon,' she said after a little pause, 'and then come down and tell me what he says. When you've done that you'd better inquire about the place. Oh, if only I were able to see it with you!'

'So you shall directly, Sheilah,' I cried. 'You shall guide and counsel me in all I do; for you are my guardian angel, and have always been.'

'Do you mean that, Jim?' she asked very softly.

'Before God, I do,' I cried vehemently. 'Sheilah, I know now what you are to me. I know that the old brotherly affection I have felt for you all these years is dead.'

'Dead, Jim!' she cried. 'Oh, surely not dead!'

'Yes, dead,' I answered; 'but out of its ashes has risen a greater, a nobler, a purer love than I ever believed myself capable of feeling. Sheilah, I love you with all my heart and soul, I love you more than life itself.'

She did not answer. For a minute or so there was only to be heard the chirping of the cicadas in the trees outside, and the dry rustle of the wind among the oranges bushes.

'Darling,' I said, when I found my voice once more, 'if I take this money and work as hard as any man can, is it to be for nothing? Or may I toil day and night, knowing that there is a reward, greater than any money, saving up for me at the end? Sheilah, do you love me well enough to be my wife!'

This time she answered, without a falter in her voice, and as she did she took my great brown hand between hers and smoothed it.

'Jim, I have always loved you' she said, 'all my life long. I will gladly; nay, that doesn't seem to express it at all. Let me say only that I love you, and that I will be your wife whenever you come to claim me. Will that satisfy you, dear?'

I bent over and kissed her on her sweet, pure lips.

'God bless you, Sheilah,' I replied so softly that I scarcely knew my own voice.

Then we both sat silent again for some time. Sheilah it was who spoke first.

'Now, Jim, how are you going to begin?'

'I'm going to find your father, and tell him everything,' I said. 'He ought to know before anyone else.'

'Very well, find him and tell him. Then go and see your own father and ask him for the money. After that, if you like, you may come back here and tell me how you have succeeded.'

I bade her good-bye, and went off to find her father.

He was in the act of leaving the stockyard when I encountered him, and I suppose he must have seen from my face that I had news for him—for, when he had shaken hands with me, he stepped back to the rails and leaned against them.

'Now, James,' he said, 'what is it ye have to tell me?'

'Something I'm rather doubtful whether you'll like,' I answered, wondering how to begin.

'Supposing I can guess already,' he said, with a smile. 'Ye have been a long time with Sheilah!'

'I have been deciding a very important matter!' I replied.

'Have ye accepted her offer?'

'I have; but how do you know that she had made one?' I answered.

'We discussed it together last night,' he said. 'My Sheilah is a generous girl, and she takes a great interest in ye, James, lad.'

'Who knows that better than I?' I answered. 'And I will do my best to show her that her trust is not misplaced. But her generous loan is not the chief thing I wish to speak to you about.'

'What is the other, then?' he said, looking a little nervously at me, I thought.

'It concerns Sheilah's own happiness,' I replied. 'Mr McLeod, your daughter has promised to be my wife.'

He was more staggered by this bit of news than I had expected he would be, and for a little while gazed at me in silent amazement. At last he pulled himself together, and said solemnly,—

'This is a very serious matter.'

'I hope it is,' I replied, 'for I love Sheilah and she loves me. We are both deeply serious, and I hope you have nothing to say against it?'

'Of course, if ye both love each other—as I believe ye do,' he answered, 'and ye, laddie, work hard to prove yourself worthy of her, I shall say nothing. But we must look things squarely in the face and have no half measures. Ye must bear with me, lad—if in what I'm going to say I hurt your feelings—but my duty lies before me, and I must do it. Ye see, Jim, ye have been foolish; your reputation in the township is a wild one; ye admitted to me having been a gambler; remember ye rode in that race against your father's and your best friends' wishes; ye were mixed up with a very disreputable set hereabouts, one of whom has been openly accused of felony; remember, I do not believe that ye had anything at all to do with the stealing of that horse—if he was stolen, as folks say; and now ye have also been turned out of house and home by your own father. Ye must yourself admit that these circumstances are not of a kind calculated to favourably impress a father who loves his only daughter as I love mine. But, on the other hand, my lad, I have known ye pretty nearly all your life, and I know that your errors are of the head, not of the heart, so I am inclined to regard them rather differently. Now, your path lies before ye. Ye have an opportunity of retrieving the past and building up the future, let us see what ye can do. If, we'll say, by this day year ye have proved to me that ye are really in earnest, ye shall have my darling, and God's blessing be on ye both. I can't say anything fairer than that, can I ?'

'I have no right to expect that you should say anything so fair,' I answered. 'Mr McLeod, I will try; come what may, you shall not be disappointed in me.'

'I believe ye, laddie,' he said, and then we went towards the front gate together. I wished him good-bye, and having done so, left him and went up the hill towards the township.

Never in my life do I remember to have walked with so proud and so confident a step. My heart was filled with hope and happiness. Sheilah loved me, and had promised to be my wife. Her father had, to all intents and purposes, given his consent. It only remained for me to prove myself worthy of the trust that had been reposed in me. And come what might, I would be worthy. Henceforward, no man should have the right to breathe a word against me. I would work for Sheilah as no man ever worked for a girl before; so that in the happy days before us she might always have reason to look up to and be proud of me. Then in a flash came back the memory of that gruesome ride to the Blackfellow's Well. Once again I saw the murdered man lying so still in

his lonely grave among the rocks on the hillside. I shuddered, and with an effort I put
the memory from me. And just as I did so,
I arrived at the hotel.

As soon as I had eaten my lunch I set
off to call upon my father. I found him
sitting in the verandah, as usual, reading. He
did not seem at all surprised at my appearance. On the other hand, he said, as I came
up to the steps,—

'You have thought better of it and come
back for that money, I suppose?'

'I have,' I answered. 'A chance has been
given me to-day of settling down to a good
thing, if I can only raise a certain sum of
money. If you are still of the same mind
as you were yesterday, I should feel grateful if you would let me have your cheque for
the amount you mentioned?'

Without another word he rose and went
into the house; when he returned he held
between his finger and thumb a little slip
of pale blue paper which I well knew was a
cheque. Giving it to me he said,—

'There it is. Now go!'

I thanked him, and turned to do as he
ordered, but before I had time to descend
the steps he stopped me by saying,—

'I have asked no questions, but I trust this business you are now embarking on will prove a little more reputable than that in which you have been hitherto engaged.'

'You need have no fear on that score,' I answered. 'At the same time, I do not admit that there was anything in the last matter, to which you refer, of which I need be ashamed.'

'I think we have discussed that before. We need not do so again.'

I was once more about to leave him, when something induced me to say,—

'Father, is this state of things to go on between us much longer? Will you never forgive a bit of heedless obstinacy on the part of one so much younger than yourself?'

'When I see signs of improvement I may be induced to re-consider my decision, not till then,' he answered. 'The sad part of it is that so far those signs are entirely wanting.'

'I am turning over a new leaf now.'

'I desire to see proof of it first,' he replied. 'I must confess my experience makes me sceptical.'

'It is useless, then, for me to say any more on the subject.'

'Quite useless. For the future let your actions speak for themselves. They will be quite significant enough, believe me.'

'Then I wish you good day.'

'Good day to you.'

And so we parted.

Leaving the old home, I strode down the hill, crossed the ford, and made my way to the principal bank in the township, where I opened an account with my father's cheque. This business completed, I passed on to the agent who had Merriman's selection under offer, and when I left his office an hour later I was in a fair way towards calling myself the proprietor of the property for a term of years.

Next morning I rode over to the selection and thoroughly examined it. It was about 10,000 acres in extent, splendidly grassed, and had an excellent frontage to the river. Merriman had built himself a hut on a little knoll, and there I determined to install myself, utilising all the time I could spare from my work among the stock in building another and better one, to which I could bring Sheilah when she became my wife. That afternoon the arrangements advanced another step, and by the end of the week following the papers were signed, and I was duly installed as possessor.

The next business was to secure the services of a man. This accomplished, I set to work in grim earnest, the fences were thoroughly overhauled and renovated—a new well was sunk in the back country—a new stockyard was erected near the hut, and, by the time Sheilah was able to get about again, I had bought a couple of thousand sheep at a price which made them an undoubted bargain, had erected my bough-shearing shed, and was all ready for getting to work upon my clip.

CHAPTER VIII

A VISIT FROM WHISPERING PETE

THREE months later the shearing of my small flock was at an end, and the result, an excellent clip, had been dispatched to market. Then, having a good deal of spare time on my hands, I held a consultation with Sheilah, planned our house, and set to work upon it. Like my own old home, it was to be of *pisa*, would consist of five rooms and a kitchen, and have a broad verandah running all round it. No man, who has not built a house under similar circumstances, will be able properly to understand what the construction of that humble abode meant to me, and how I worked at it. Every second that I could possibly spare was given to it, and as bit by bit it raised itself above the earth, my love for Sheilah seemed to grow stronger and purer with it. It was a proud day for me, you may

be sure, when the roof was started, and a still
prouder when it was completed. The windows and doors were then put into the walls,
the floors of the rooms and verandah laid, the
papering and painting completed, until at last it
stood ready for occupation. A prettier position
no man could possibly have desired, and as far
as construction went, well, when I say that
I had worked at it with the patience and
thoroughness that can only be brought to
bear by a man in what is a labour of love, you
will have some idea of what it was like. Ah !
what a glorious time that was—when everything
animate and inanimate spoke to me of Sheilah.
When I rose from my bed in the morning, with
the sun, it was to work for her, and when I
returned to it again at night it was with the
knowledge that I had done all that man
could do for her, and was just so many
hours nearer the time when she would be my
wife. It may be a strange way of putting it,
but if you've ever been in love yourself you'll
understand me when I say that her gentle
influence was with me always, in the wind
blowing through the long bush grass, in the
whispering of the leaves of the trees, in the
rising of the moon above the distant ranges,
and in the murmur of the water in the

creek. Nor did I want for encouragement. When the day's work was done I would cross the creek and discuss it with my sweetheart and her father, and even Colin McLeod, now that it was all definitely settled between us and he knew his fate, treated me quite as one of the family, and without a sign of his old antagonism.

Then, at last, the joyful day was fixed, and I knew that on a certain Thursday two months ahead, all being well, Sheilah would become my wife. The house was completely finished, painted, papered, and furnished, and even the garden, which I had constructed so that it should slope down to the river, was beginning to show signs of the labour that had been expended on it. Then, in the midst of my happiness, when I felt so secure that it seemed as if nothing could possibly come between me and the woman I loved, something happened which was destined to be the precursor of all the terrible things I have yet to tell, and which were to bow Sheilah's head and mine in sorrow and shame down even to the very dust.

It was a night at the end of the first week after the completion of the new house. Having finished his supper, my factotum had

gone across to the township, and I was pay-
ing my evening visit to Sheilah. About
ten o'clock I started for home. It had been
hot and thundery all the afternoon and evening, and now a mass of heavy cloud had
almost covered the heavens. The wind
whistled dismally through the she-oak trees
in the scrub and moaned along the valley.
A premonition of coming ill was upon me,
and when I reached the new house, where
I had already installed myself, I went into
the kitchen feeling ready to jump away from
my own shadow. The fire just showed a
red glow, and to my amazement gave me the
outline of a man sitting beside it.

'You're up late, Dick,' I cried, thinking
it was my man returned from his evening's
outing. But he did not answer.

I lit a candle and held it aloft. Then I
almost dropped it in horror and astonishment.

The man sitting beside the fire was
Whispering Pete!

'Good heavens, how did you get here?'
I cried, as I set the candle down upon the
table.

'Rode,' he answered laconically, getting
on to his feet. 'My horse is in your stock-

yard now. I've ridden three hundred miles this week, and must be over the border before Tuesday.'

'But why have you come here of all other places?' I asked, resolved to let him see that I was not at all pleased to have him on my premises.

'Because I had to see you, Jim, for myself.' Here he stopped and went over to the door and looked out. 'Nobody about is there?' he asked suspiciously.

'Not a soul,' I answered. 'Go on, out with it, what do you want to see me for?

He came closer and sank his voice almost to a whisper, as he said,—

'Because, Jim, if we're not careful there'll be trouble, and what's more, big trouble. The police are looking high and low for Jarman, and naturally they can't find him. The rumour which I had circulated that he followed the horse Gaybird up to Northern Queensland has been exploded, and now they're coming back to the original idea—that we know something of his whereabouts.'

'Don't say "we" if you please,' I answered hotly. 'Remember I had nothing at all to do with it.'

Once more he leant towards me. This time he spoke in the same curious undertone, but with more emphasis.

'Indeed, and pray who had then? Jim Heggarstone, if you're wise you won't try that game with me. It will not do. Just review the circumstances of the case, my friend, before you talk like that. What horse did you ride in that race? Why, the horse that was discovered to have been stolen. Where did you spend the evening after the race? In my house. Jarman was among the guests, wasn't he? Who took his dead body away and buried it in the mountains, and then disappeared himself? Why, you did. Are those the actions of an innocent man? Answer me that question before you say anything more about having had nothing to do with it!'

I saw it all, then, with damning distinctness. And oh, how I loathed myself for the part I had played in it.

'You have contrived my ruin, Pete!' I cried, like a man in agony.

'Don't be a fool,' he answered. 'I only tell you this to show you that we must stand by each other, and sink or swim together. If they ask me, I shall admit that he dined

with us and went away about ten o'clock.
I should advise you to do the same. If you
did your work well they can hunt till all's
blue and they'll not find the body. And as
long as they can't find that we're safe. I
came out of my way here to warn you,
because inquiries are certain to be made,
and then we must all give the same answer.
Present a bold front to them, or else
clear out or do away with yourself altogether.'

I could say nothing — I was too stunned
even to think. I wanted air and to be alone,
so I opened the door, and went out into the
night. The wind had dropped and an un-
earthly stillness reigned, broken at intervals
by the sullen booming of thunder in the
west. It was a night surcharged with
tragedy, and surely my situation was tragic
enough to satisfy anybody.

'And where are you going to now,
Pete?' I asked, when I went into the room
again.

'I'm off to Sydney,' he replied. 'I shall
show myself there as much as possible, for
I do not want it to be supposed that I am
in hiding. Then I shall wait awhile, and,
when things get settled down a bit, clear

out of Australia altogether. If you are wise, I should advise you to do the same!'

'Never!' I answered firmly. Then, after a little pause, I continued, 'Pete, does it never strike you what a cruel wrong you have done me? Fancy, if the girl I am about to marry — whom I love better than my life — should hear of my part in this dreadful business? Imagine what she should think of me?'

'She would think all the more of you,' he answered quickly. 'Remember you are sacrificing yourself for your friend, and as long as it doesn't make any difference to them, women like that sort of thing.' Then, changing his voice a little, he said, 'Jim, you must not think I'm ungrateful. If ever the chance serves I'll set it right for you—I give you my word I will.'

He held out his hand to me, but I would not take it. It seemed to me to reek with the blood of the murdered man.

'You won't take my hand?—well, perhaps you're right. But I tell you this, man, if you think I haven't repented the stab that killed him, you're making the greatest mistake of your life. My God! that poor devil's cry, to say nothing of the expression on his face as he fell back in his chair, has been a nightmare to me ever since. I never go to sleep without dreaming of him. Out there, in the loneliness of the West, I've had him with me day and night. Think what that means, and then see if you can judge me too harshly.'

'God help you!' I cried. 'I cannot judge you!'

'And you will help to save me, Jim,' he said, with infinite pleading in his voice. 'You will not draw any tighter the rope that is round my throat—will you?'

'What do you mean by drawing it tighter?'

'I mean, you will not say or do anything that may lead them to suspect?'

'What do you take me for?' I cried. 'I am not an informer. No; I will do my best for you, come what may. But, remember this, Pete, I'll not have you coming round here any more. It isn't safe.'

'I'll remember it, never fear,' he answered. 'You shall not set eyes on me again. Now I'll lie down for an hour, and then I must be off.'

There and then he laid himself down on my kitchen floor near the wall, and in less than five minutes was fast asleep, for all the world as if he had not a care upon his mind.

I sat by the window, thinking and thinking. What a position was I in! Just as I had thought myself clear of my old life for ever, it had sprung up again, hydra-headed, and threatened to annihilate me. A deadly fear was tearing at my heart-strings; not fear for myself, you must understand that, but fear for Sheilah — Sheilah, who believed in me so implicitly.

At the end of an hour, almost to the minute, Pete sat up, rubbed his eyes, and then leapt to his feet.

'Time's up,' he said briskly. 'I must be getting on again. Will you come down to the yard with me?'

'Of course,' I answered, and followed him out of the door. We walked across the paddock together, and when his horse was saddled, he turned to me and said, solemnly,—

'As you deal by me, Jim, so may God deal with you! I'm not the sort of chap you would associate with religion, but, little though you may be able to square it with what you know of me, I tell you I am a firm believer in a God. My account with Him is a pretty black one, I'm afraid; but yours, old man, is made a bit whiter by what you've done, and will do for me—there's a sermon for you!   Now, good-bye; perhaps we may never meet again.'

'Good-bye,' I answered, and this time, almost without knowing it, I shook him by the hand.   Then he swung himself into his saddle, and without another word drove in his spurs and galloped off into the darkness. I stood and watched him till I could see him no longer, then back I went to the house, my heart full of forebodings.   Try how I would, I could not drive the memory of his visit out of my mind.   An unknown, yet all-consuming, terror seized me at every sound. I thought of the lonely grave among the rocks near the Blackfellow's Well, of the mysterious man in grey who had appeared, no one knew whence, to relieve me of the horse on that awful night.   Then I fell to wondering what Sheilah and her father would say if they knew all.   I never thought of bed.   Indeed, when the sun rose, he found me still gazing into the ash-strewn fireplace thinking and thinking the same interminable thoughts.

That afternoon Sheilah commented on my haggard appearance, and I had to invent an excuse to account for it.   Then under her gentle influence my fears slowly subsided, until I had forgotten them as much as it would ever again be possible for me to do.

On the Thursday following Pete's visit, I wrote to my father informing him of my approaching marriage and imploring him to make the occasion an opportunity for a reconciliation. To my letter I received the following characteristic reply :—

'SIR,—I have to acknowledge the receipt of your communication of yesterday's date, and to thank you for the same. In reply, I beg to state that I have noted the contents as ·you desire me to do. With regard to the step you intend taking, as it has been arranged without any consideration of my feelings, I am not prepared to venture an opinion of its merits. As to the latter portion of your communication, I may say that on and after your wedding-day I shall be pleased to consider you once more a member of my family.—I am, Your paternal parent,

'MARMADUKE HEGGARSTONE.

'P.S.—I may say that I have in my possession certain jewels which were the property of your mother, and which are heirlooms in our family. On your wedding-day I shall, according to custom, do myself the honour of begging your wife's acceptance of them.'

CHAPTER IX

A FORTNIGHT before my wedding-day it became necessary for me to send a small mob of cattle away to Bourke, and as I had no drover, and could not afford to wait for one to put in an appearance, I determined to take them down myself. Accordingly, having bidden Sheilah good-bye, off I went, and, after what seemed an eternity, delivered them to the agent and paid the cheque I received in return into the bank to my account. Then, with a joyful heart, I turned my horse's head towards home once more. The journey back was a quicker one than it had been going, and only occupied four days. Night was falling as I reached the township, and as soon as I had turned my horses loose and snatched a hasty meal, I changed my clothes and crossed the creek to McLeod's homestead. It was the night before my wedding-day, and with a wave of happiness flooding my heart I shut the gate behind me and went up the path. A warm glow of lamplight streamed from the window of the sitting-room, and as the blind had not been drawn, I could see Sheilah, her father and Colin McLeod sitting talking earnestly together at the table. The solemn expressions on their faces frightened me, though I could not tell why, and it was with almost a feeling of nervousness that I pushed open the door and walked into the room.

When I entered there was a little embarrassed silence for a moment, and then Sheilah came across the room and kissed me before them all and wished me joy of being home again. Both old McLeod and Colin then shook me by the hand, but it seemed as if there were something they were keeping back from me. I passed with Sheilah to the other end of the room, and stood leaning against the mantlepiece waiting for the matter to be explained to me. It was Sheilah who spoke first. She stood beside me, and, taking my hand, said to her father,—

'Dad, dear, do not let us beat about the bush. Tell Jim straightforwardly what is said about him.'

I pricked up my ears and felt a chill like that of death pass over me. What was coming now? I asked myself. Old McLeod rose from his chair as if he were going to make a speech, while Colin looked another way.

'James, my lad,' said the old man, 'ye must forgive us for ever listening to such talk on the eve of your wedding-day, but we will trust to your good sense to understand why we do it. Remember, none of us believe it. But we feel we ought to have your word against those who are hinting things against ye.'

'What is it they are saying against me?' I asked, my heart fairly standing still with fear of what his answer would be.

Old McLeod paused for a moment, and then, looking me full in the face, said,—

'James, while ye have been away inquiries have been made concerning the disappearance of the Sydney detective, Jarman, who was here at the time of the races last year, and who has never since been heard of.'

'But what has that got to do with me?' I asked, feeling all the time that my face must be giving damning evidence against me. 'Do they accuse me of having murdered him, or what?'

'No, no! Not quite as bad as that! But

they say he was last seen walking through
the township towards Whispering Pete's house
in your company; and that he has never been
seen since.'

'Of course, he was seen with me,' I said.
'He dined and spent the evening with us
at Pete's house.   But I don't see anything
suspicious in that—do you?'

'Not at all,' said the old man.   'But what
became of him afterwards?'

'How can I tell you?' I cried impatiently.
'I was told that he went after the horse up
North.   He did not make me his confidant.
Why should he?   I had never seen him be-
fore that day, and I have never seen him
since.'

'Don't be angry with father for telling
you what people say, Jim, dear,' said Sheilah,
looking into my face with her beautiful eyes.
'Remember, none of us have ever doubted
you for a moment.'

'Thank God for that, Sheilah,' I answered.
'It would not be like you to believe ill of
an innocent man.'

Colin McLeod was the next to speak, and
what he said was to the point—straightforward
and honourable, like himself.

'Heggarstone,' said he, 'in my official

capacity I have to follow any instructions that are given to me; but I want you to understand that personally I do not believe you had any hand in the man's disappearance.'

'Thank you, Colin,' I said. 'I don't believe you do.'

Old McLeod seemed to me to be considering something in his mind, for presently he turned from looking out of the window and said,—

'James, it's a nasty thing to ask ye to do. But I do it for motives of my own. Here is a Bible.' He took one down from a shelf and laid it on the table before me. 'For form's sake, will ye swear on it that ye know nothing of, and had nothing to do with, the disappearance of this man? It will make my mind easier if ye will, because, then, I can give your accusers the lie direct.'

I looked from the old man to the open Bible, then at Sheilah, then last at Colin. But before I could do anything, Sheilah had sprung forward and snatched up the Bible, crying, as she did so, 'No! no! There shall be no swearing. I won't have it. Jim's word is the word of a God-fearing, honest man, and we'll take that or nothing. Then, turning to me, she said, 'Jim, you will tell them, on your love for me, that you know nothing of the matter, won't you, dear?'

The room seemed to rock and swing round me. A black mist was rising before my eyes. I was conscious only that I was lost; that I was about to lie, and wilfully lie, to the one woman of all others that I wanted to think well of me. What could I do? If I refused to tell them I would be giving assent to the charges brought against me, and in that case send Pete to the gallows, while, by being compelled to give her up, I should break Sheilah's heart. If I perjured myself and swore that I knew nothing, then some day the truth might come out; and what would happen then? Like a flash up came the remembrance of Pete's visit, and my oath to him. Already I felt that they were wondering at my silence. Oh, the agony of those moments! Then I made up my mind; and, taking Sheilah's hand, lifted it to my lips, and said deliberately, with a full knowledge of what I was doing—but with every word cutting deeper and deeper into my heart,—

'I swear, by my love for you, Sheilah, that I know nothing of the man's fate.' Then she pulled my face down to hers and kissed me before them all.

'Jim,' she said, 'you know that I never doubted you.'

The others shook me by the hand, and then, after a few words about the arrangements for the morrow, I said good night and went home. But I went like a man who did not know where he was going. I took no heed of my actions, but walked on and on—turning neither to the right hand nor to the left—conscious only of my degradation, of my lie to Sheilah. I was ruined! Ruined! Ruined! That was my one thought. Then, arriving at the river bank, I threw myself down upon the ground, and cried like a little child. Never shall I be able to rid my mind of the memory of that agonising night. From long before midnight till the stars were paling in the east, preparatory to dawn, I lay just where I had dropped, hopeless even unto death! All joy had gone out of existence for me. And this was my wedding-day—the day that should have been the happiest of my life.

Gradually the darkness departed from the sky, and in the chill grey of dawn I rose to my feet, and, worn and weary past all belief, like a hunted criminal fearing to be seen by his fellow-man, I crept down to the water's edge and laved my burning face. Then, ford-ing the river higher up, I went back to my home. There, in the morning sunlight, stood the pretty house I had built, surrounded by the garden on which I had expended so much loving thought and care. On the posts of the verandah and along the eastern wall the geranium creeper was just beginning to climb. My dog came from his kennel near the wood heap and fawned upon me; my favourite horse whinnied to me from the slip panels near the stockyard gate; everything seemed happy and full of the joy of living—only I, who by rights should have been happiest of them all, was miserable. I stooped and patted the dog, and then went into the house. In every room was the pretty furniture of which Sheilah and I were so proud. The dining-room, with its neat appointments, seemed to mock me; the drawing-room, in the corner of which stood Sheilah's piano, sent over the previous day, turned upon me in mute reproach. All the happiness of my life called me coward and liar, and taunted me with my shame. I went into my bedroom and looked at myself in the glass. I could hardly believe that it was my own face I saw reflected there, so drawn and haggard was it. As it was not yet five o'clock, I threw myself upon my bed and tried to sleep;

but it was impossible. I could do nothing but think. Over and over last night's scene I went; with horrible distinctness every circumstance rose before me. At last I could bear it no longer; so I got up and went out of the house again. And this was my wedding-morn. God help me! My wedding-morn!

In ten hours—for the ceremony was fixed for three o'clock in the afternoon—I should be standing by Sheilah's side to swear before God and man that I would take her into my keeping, that I would love and cherish her all the days of my life. How had I already shown my love for her? How had I cherished her? Oh, wretched, wretched man that I was! It were better for me that I should die before I took that vow!

In an attempt to discover some relief from my awful thoughts I set myself some work, fed the animals, milked the cow, boiled myself some water, and made a cup of tea; and then, finding that it was not yet eight o'clock, I caught a horse and rode off into the back country. How far I went I could not say, for I took no heed of time or distance. But it must have been a good journey, for when I returned to the homestead my horse was completely knocked up. By this time it was one o'clock, and I knew that in another hour I should have to begin my preparations for the ceremony. A bath somewhat revived me, and I passed to my bedroom, where my wedding suit lay staring at me from the bed, feeling a little refreshed. By half-past two I was ready and waiting for the kind-hearted storekeeper I have mentioned before, and whom I had asked to act as my best man. I dreaded his coming, for some unknown reason; yet when I heard his firm step upon the path it seemed to brace me like a tonic. I called him into the house.

'Good luck to you,' he said, as he entered and shook me by the hand. 'If ever a man deserves a change of fortune, you're that one. Heaven knows you've worked hard enough for it.'

'It's about time, for hitherto luck hasn't run my way, has it?' I answered bitterly.

'Hullo!' he cried, looking at me in surprise. 'This is not the sort of humour to be in on your wedding-day. Jim, my boy, if I didn't happen to know that you love the girl you are going to marry with your whole heart and soul, I should feel a bit concerned about you.'

'Yes, you know I love her, don't you?' I answered, as if I desired that point to be re-assured on by an independent witness. 'There can be no possible doubt about my love for

Sheilah—God bless her! But I'm afraid!—horribly afraid.'

'Of what?' he asked; then, mistaking my meaning, 'but, there, it's only natural. They say every bridegroom's afraid.'

'Then God help every bridegroom who feels as I do—that's all I can say.'

'Come, come,' he said, picking up his hat, 'this won't do at all. I can't have you talking like this. Anyhow, we had better be off. It's close upon a quarter to three now, and it would never do to keep them waiting.'

Accordingly we passed out of the house, and set off for the church, which stood on a little hill above the township. All through that walk I stumbled along like one in a dream, talking always with feverish eagerness, afraid even to trust myself to think of what I said. For was I not marrying Sheilah with a lie upon my lips?

As it happened, we were the first to arrive at the church, so we went inside and waited. Presently others began to put in an appearance, until by three o'clock the little church was well filled. A few moments later there was a turning of heads, and a whisper went about that the bride was arriving. By this time I was trembling like a leaf, and, I don't doubt, looked more like a man about to be hanged than a bridegroom waiting for his bride. Then the doors were pushed open, and in a stream of sunshine Sheilah, dressed all in white, entered leaning on her father's arm. When she got half-way up the aisle I went down to meet her, and we walked to the altar rails, where the old clergyman was waiting for us, together. Then the ceremony commenced.

When the last words were spoken, I, James, had taken Sheilah to be my wedded wife, for better for worse, for richer for poorer, in sickness and in health, swearing to love her and to cherish her, till death should us part. The good old man gave us his blessing, and then, with my bride upon my arm, I passed down the aisle again towards the porch. The greatest event of my life was celebrated, Sheilah and I were man and wife.

The little crowd, gathered on either side of the porch, parted to let us through, and we were in the act of turning down the path which would bring us out opposite McLeod's gate, when I was conscious of a tall figure in uniform coming towards me. It was Sergeant Burns, chief of the township police. He came up and stood before us—then, placing his hand upon my shoulder, said,—

'James Heggarstone, in the Queen's name, I arrest you on a charge of murder. I warn you that anything you may say will be used as evidence against you.'

Darkness seemed suddenly to fall upon me but before it enveloped me completely I saw the crowd draw closer to us. I felt Sheilah slip from my side and fall, with a little moan, to the ground. After that I remember no more of what happened, till I woke to find myself in a cell at the police station, feeling the most miserable man in the whole scheme of the universe.

The blow had fallen at last.

CHAPTER X

IT was strange, but nevertheless a fact, how to be accounted for I do not know, that when I came to my senses again and found myself in the cell at the police station, I was easier in my mind than I had been at all since Pete's visit to my house. The truth was the blow had fallen and my mind was set at rest once and for all. At first I was like a man dead, but now that my wits had returned to me, I was like a man who had still to die. Of Sheilah I dared not think.

About sundown the Sergeant entered my cell and found me lying on the rough bed-place with my face turned to the wall. He had known me since I was a boy, and it didn't take much to see that he was really sorry for me.

'Come, come, Jim, my lad,' he said kindly, walking over and sitting down on the bed beside me. 'Don't give way like this. Look your difficulties in the face and meet them with a bold front like a man.'

'It's all very well for you to say meet them with a bold front,' I answered, sitting up and looking at him. 'But think what all this means to me.'

'I know about that, my poor lad,' he replied. 'And there's not a soul but is down-right sorry for you. Unfortunately we had no option but to arrest you as we did. We received our instructions by telegraph from Brisbane.'

'But what made you arrest me?' I asked. 'Surely they're not going to try to prove me guilty of the murder of this man?'

'I can't tell you anything about that, of course,' he answered. 'But we had to arrest you, and as you are to be brought before the magistrates first thing to-morrow morning you'll know then. In the mean-time, if you want to send for a lawyer, you are, of course, at liberty to do so!'

'I'll do so at once then,' I answered eagerly, clutching, like a drowning man, at the straw held out to me. 'I'd like to have Mr Perkins if you will let him know. And might I have some paper, pens, and ink? I must write some letters.'

'Of course, you can have anything you want in reason,' the Sergeant answered. 'Remember, Jim, you're innocent until you're proved guilty.'

When he went away he did not forget to send in the things I had asked for, and as soon as I had received them I sat down and wrote a letter to Sheilah. With a mind that was not nearly as easy as I tried to make it appear, I told her to keep up her heart, and tried to make her believe that this absurd charge must be quickly disproved, as, indeed, I confidently expected it would be. Even if the stigma should remain upon my character, they could never convict me of connivance for want of evidence. As long as the grave under the rocks remained undiscovered, all would be well. By this time Pete was probably in America, and the One-eyed Doctor with him. The man who had taken the horse from me at the corner fence could say nothing about the body, because he had not seen it. So that in any case I could scarcely fail to be acquitted. With this idea firmly implanted in my mind, I described my arrest as the only possible result of all the malicious reports that had lately been circulated concerning me, and even went so far as to say that I was glad the business had been brought to a head at last. What was more, I stated that I felt so far convinced of the result as to arrange to meet her the following day—after the examination before the magistrates—when we could enter our new home together freed of all false charges and suspicions. How far my hopes were destined to be realised you will see for yourself.

During the afternoon Mr Perkins, a solicitor who had done two or three little bits of legal business for me in brighter days, arrived at the station, and was immediately brought to me. He was a sharp, ferrety-faced little fellow, with a bald head, clean-shaven chin and upper lip, and bushy grey eyebrows. He had a big knowledge of Colonial law, and had the wit to remain in the country, quietly working up an enormous business for himself, when so many of his fraternity were rushing to the cities to take their chances of losing or making fortunes there. He seated himself on a stool near the door, and, while doing so, expressed himself as exceedingly sorry to see me in such an unpleasant position. Then, taking his note-book from his pocket, he set himself to ask me a few questions.

'I understand that you are prepared to admit having seen the man Jarman on the day of the race in question?' he began.

'Quite prepared,' I answered. 'I was introduced to him immediately after I had weighed out!'

'By whom was this introduction effected, and at what spot?'

'By Whispering Pete,' I replied. 'And alongside the refreshment bar at the back of the grand stand.'

'And he dined with you a couple of hours later, I understand. At whose invitation?'

'At Whispering Pete's, of course. It was his house.'

'To be sure. Now think for one moment before you answer the question I am going to ask you. Were you present when Whispering Pete invited him? And what words did he use, to the best of your recollection?'

'It came about in this way. We had finished our drinks and were moving along the track that leads up to the township, when Jarman said he was sorry the amusement was all over, as there was nothing to do in a little up-country township like ours in the evening. Then Pete said, "Well, if you're afraid of being dull why not come up and dine with us?" "I'll do so with pleasure," said Jarman, and then we started off for home.'

'That was exactly what occurred, to the very best of your remembrance?'

'It was. I think I have given you an exact description of it.'

'And when you reached Pete's house—you sat down to dinner, I suppose?'

'Not at once. We each had a glass of sherry first, and sat for a while in the verandah.'

'After which you went in to dinner? Next to whom did Jarman sit?'

'Between Pete and myself.'

'Was he in good spirits, think you? Did he seem to be enjoying himself? I am not asking these questions out of idle curiosity— you will of course understand that.'

'In excellent spirits. He told several good stories, described two or three sensational arrests he had made in his career, and I should say enjoyed himself very much.'

'And after dinner? What did you do then?'

'We sat at the table smoking and talking —then I rose to go.'

'Leaving them still at the table, I presume? Please be particular in your answer.'

'Yes, they were still at the table. I bade them good-night, and then started for home.'

'Had you any reason for going away at that moment? By the way, what time was it when you said good-bye to them?'

'Ten o'clock exactly. I remember looking at my watch and thinking how quickly the evening had passed.'

'And what was your reason for going?'

'I could hardly tell you, I'm afraid. You see I was expecting trouble with my father because I had ridden the horse for Pete, and I wanted to get the fuss over and done with as soon as possible.'

'And when you reached your home, what happened?'

'I saw my father, and we had a violent quarrel. He ordered me out of his house then and there, and I went.'

'Where did you go?'

'I went back to Pete, having nowhere else to go.'

'And when you got there was Jarman still there?'

I stopped for a second. This was the question I had all along been dreading. But

I had no option. If I was going to keep my plighted word, and Pete was to be saved, I could not tell the truth. So I said,—

'He had gone.'

'Did you see him go—or meet him on the road?'

'No. I am quite sure I did not.'

'And when you were alone with Pete and the other man, Finnan, what did you do?'

'I told Pete what a nasty fix I was in, and let him see that my father had turned me out of doors for riding The Unknown.'

'You still consider, then, that the horse was The Unknown—and not the Gaybird, as people assert?'

'I cannot say. I never saw Gaybird. I only know that Pete told me his horse's name was The Unknown, and having no reason to doubt his veracity, that satisfied me, and I asked no further questions?'

'I see! And what had Pete to say when you told him your condition?'

'He said he was extremely sorry to hear it, and asked how he could help me.'

'And what answer did you give him?'

'I told him that he could best help me by finding something for me to do. I said I was not going to remain in the township idle, to be gaped at and talked about by everybody.'

'A very proper spirit. And I understand Pete said he would find you something?'

'Yes. He told me he had a mob of cattle then on the way to Sydney. He had had to put a man in charge who was not quite up to the work, and then he went on to say that if I liked to have the post I was welcome to it. He said he thought, if I looked sharp, I could catch them up by daybreak.'

'So you started off there and then to try and overtake them?'

'Not at once. I had on my best clothes, you see; so I went home again, crept in by a side window, changed my things, got a stock whip, packed a few odds and ends into a valise, and then rejoined Pete, who had a saddle-horse and a pack-horse waiting for me by the creek. Then off I went, and by riding hard caught the mob just as day was breaking.'

'Well, if that is exactly what happened,' said the worthy old lawyer, 'I really think I can get you off.'

'I hope and pray you may. Fancy being arrested on such a charge on your wedding-day. How would you have liked that, Mr Perkins?'

'Provided it happened before the ceremony, and they did not lock me up for more than ten years, I should think it the most fortunate thing that could befall me,' he answered. And as he said it I remembered that he was a confirmed woman-hater.

Shaking me by the hand, he left me, and I sat down again to my thoughts. But my reverie was soon interrupted by the re-appearance of the Sergeant.

'There is a lady here who wishes to see you,' he said, and forthwith ushered Sheilah into my cell. Then, softly closing the door behind him, he left us together. Sheilah ran into my arms, and for some minutes sobbed upon my shoulder. When she had recovered her composure a little, I led her to a seat and sat down beside her.

'Sheilah — my poor little wife,' I said, with my arm round her neck, 'to think that I should have been separated from you like this on our wedding-day. But we must be brave, little wife, mustn't we?'

'Oh, Jim! My poor Jim,' was all she could say in answer. 'You are innocent. I know you are innocent. Oh, why are they so cruel as to bring this charge against you?'

'Of course I am innocent, darling,' I replied, kissing her tear-stained cheeks. 'I would not have laid a finger upon the man to hurt him for all the world. But you need have no fear. I have Perkins's word for it that he can get me off. He has just left me after asking half-a-hundred questions.'

'But if the man was not murdered as they say, he must be alive at this moment, and in that case he will be sure to come forward and clear your character.'

'Of course he will, if he's alive. But, thank goodness, I think I shall be able to clear myself without troubling him.'

'Pray God you may. Oh, Jim, I feel like an old woman instead of a young bride. I have been so ill all the afternoon that my father would not let me come to you before. But I am going to be brave now, and to-morrow I shall have you with me again. Then I will make it up to you for all the misery you are suffering now.'

'Who knows that better than I do, my darling.'

She rose to her feet, and then, stooping, kissed me on the forehead.

'My own true husband,' she said, 'I believe in you before all the world, remember that. Now I must be going. But first, my father is outside. May he come in?'

'I should like to see him before all others,'

I said—and she went to the door. The officer outside opened it for her, and next moment old McLeod entered and shook me by the hand.

'I wonder that you care to do this,' I said, as I returned his salutation. 'I hope it shows me that so far you do not believe me guilty of the horrible charge they have brought against me?'

'I do not!' he answered stoutly. 'No, James, my lad, in Sheilah and myself ye have two stalwart champions.'

'And I thank God for it,' I replied fervently. 'I will repay it you both, as you will see, when I am released.'

The time was soon up for them to leave, so bidding me good-bye, they went out, and once more the heavy door closed upon me. But they had done that which had cheered me and made me happier than I had been for some time past. Half-an-hour later my tea was brought to me, and by eight o'clock I was in bed and asleep. For the reason that I had had no rest at all on the previous night, I slept like a top now—a heavy dreamless slumber that lasted well into next morning. In fact, it must have been considerably after six o'clock before I opened my eyes. Then for a moment I was puzzled to know where I was, but my memory soon returned to me, and the recollection of the arrest and all that had followed it rushed back upon me. However, I was quite confident that in another few hours I should be at liberty, so my present captivity and inconvenience might only be regarded as temporary, and, therefore, easily to be borne. Outside the cell window the birds were chirping merrily, and now and again I could hear the voices of passers-by. Giving up an attempt to hear what they said, I began to wonder what Sheilah was doing, and whether she was as anxious to see me as I was to see her.

Then breakfast was brought in, and by the time I had finished my meal and taken some exercise in the yard it was time to be going into Court.

The Court House at Barranda adjoins the police station, so that, fortunately, I was not called upon to face the public before my case was called on. Then a constable signed to me to follow him, and I crossed the yard and went towards a narrow door. This led directly into the Court itself, and as soon as I had passed through it, I found myself standing in the centre of a large room, of which the gallery at one end and a daïs at the other were all densely crowded. A trooper opened the gate of the dock, and I immediately went up two steps and entered it. Almost every face in the Court was familiar to me, and the magistrate on the Bench I had known ever since I was a little boy. At the further end of a long form, below the daïs, I saw old McLeod sitting. Mr Perkins was just in front of him, and the Lawyer, who was to act as prosecutor for the Government, stood opposite him. Then, just as the case was about to commence, the door at the back of the Bench opened, and who should appear but my father. He looked very bent and old, and seemed to be labouring under the influence of some powerful excitement. He glared round the Court as a little buzz of astonishment naturally went up, and then took his place on the form where the witnesses were seated. The case then commenced. First and foremost the charge was read to me, and in reply to questions asked, I gave my name, age and address, and pleaded not guilty. A witness was then called to prove that I had ridden the horse The Unknown, supposed to be the property of, and entered in the name of Peter Dempster, in the race for the Barranda Cup, and that I was afterwards seen in the company of the missing man. The landlord of the hotel deposed that Jarman had dined out on the evening in question, and had not returned since then, either to pay his bill or to remove his effects. This evidence created a sensation, which was intensified when another witness stepped into the box, and swore that on the night in question, somewhere about half-past ten, he was taking a short cut across Pete's paddock to reach the township when he heard a sharp scream, such as would be made by a man in pain come from the direction of Dempster's house.

'And what did you do on hearing it?' asked the Lawyer, who, as I say, was conducting the prosecution.

'I stood still and listened for it again,' answered the witness.

'And did you hear it?' asked the Lawyer.

'No, not again,' replied the witness.

'And then?'

'I continued my walk towards the township.'

'You did not consider it sufficiently peculiar as to warrant your making inquiries?'

'It was so sharp and sudden that I did not know what it was.'

The Prosecuting Lawyer resumed his seat, and Mr Perkins thereupon jumped up and began to cross-examine the witness after his own fashion. When he had finished and had sat down again, he had elicited from the man—first that he could not even swear it was a human scream he heard; secondly, that it was so sudden and so short that he would hardly like to swear solemnly that he heard anything at all. It might have been, so the cross-examination elicited, the wind in the grass, a mopoke in a tree, perhaps, or a curlew down by the river side. The man could not state anything definitely, and Mr Perkins asked the Bench to severely censure the police for bringing such paltry and unreliable evidence before the Court. This was decidedly a point in my favour.

Pete's cook and housekeeper was the next witness called. After a good look at me, she asserted that she remembered seeing me sitting next to Jarman in the dining - room when she took in some hot water which had been ordered by Pete. That was about nine-thirty o'clock. The missing man, she said, was talking and laughing, and seemed to be enjoying himself immensely. When she entered a second time, about ten-fifteen, I was not present in the room, though Jarman was. She did not hear a scream, nor did she see any of the visitors leave the house. She went to bed early, having to be up by daybreak next morning to bake her bread. On being asked if she had noticed anything peculiar about the dinner, either while it was proceeding or afterwards, she answered that she had not. Thereupon a small and dirty square of linen was produced by the police and laid on the table in the centre of the Court. The witness was asked if she recognised it, and she was obliged to admit that it was a tablecloth that had once belonged to Whispering Pete. It had been discovered by the police about a week after the dinner on the edge of a burned-out bonfire. The rest of the cloth had evidently been consumed by the fire. She was next asked if she could swear to the cloth that had been used on that occasion. This she could do, she answered, on account of a small iron mould in the corner. She was thereupon shown a mark of that description in a corner of the cloth. Having recognised it, she was told to step down, and Marmaduke Heggarstone was called.

With a hasty glance at me, my parent

walked into the box and took the customary oath. In reply to the Lawyer's questions, he asserted that I had ridden the race against his wishes, and that he had promised to turn me out of his house if I did so. I rode, and when I visited him shortly after ten o'clock on the night mentioned, he acted upon his word and turned me out. At the time I was the worse for liquor, and to the best of his belief was in a very quarrelsome condition. I had remained with him about a quarter-of-an-hour. Where I had gone after that he could not say, but he had since learned from his housekeeper that I had returned to the house later and had changed my clothes. After a short cross-examination by Perkins, which elicited very little, he sat down, and old Betty, cur housekeeper, was called. She went into the box in fear and trembling, and immediately she got there began to cry. But the Lawyer was very easy with her, and in a few minutes she was able to answer his questions after her usual fashion. She deposed to hearing me come back to the house about half-past eleven, and to finding my best clothes hanging on the peg next morning when she went into my room. The Lawyer thereupon took up a coat from where it lay on the table and showed it to her.

' Do you recognise this garment?' he asked. She signified that she had seen it before.

'Where did you see it last?' he went on.

'When it was hanging up in Master Jim's room,' she said. 'Before you took it away.'

'How do you account for this stain on the left cuff? Or, perhaps, you have not yet seen it?'

The witness answered that she had noticed it on the morning following the dinner, and had intended to sponge it out, but had forgotten to do so.

Mr Perkins then cross-examined her as to the time at which she thought she had heard me re-enter the house, but he failed to shake her. When she left the box, the Government analytical chemist from Brisbane was called, and to my horror and astonishment swore that the stain upon the coat cuff was undoubtedly that of blood, and human blood. He had carefully examined it and tried it by all the known tests, and his opinion was not to be shaken. When he had finished his evidence my case had altogether changed. My tongue seemed to cleave to the roof of my parched mouth. I clung to the rail of the dock, and felt as if by this time all the world must be convinced of my guilt. I glanced at the form on which old McLeod sat, and saw that his face was ashen pale.

Then the last witness was called. He was a stranger to me. A tall, black-bearded man, with a crafty, unpleasant face. In answer to the usual questions he said his name was Bennett and that he was a settler on the Warrego River. On the day preceding the night in question, he had been in Carryfort township, when he received a letter sent by special messenger from Peter Dempster to say that he had a valuable horse which he wanted him to take charge of for a few months. A man would meet him at a certain corner of Judson's Boundary fence near the Blackfellow's well, outside Barranda township, about one in the morning, and give delivery. Yes! he had had many dealings in horses and cattle with the before-mentioned Dempster, and not liking to disappoint him in this case, camped near the place mentioned and waited for his messenger to make his appearance. At about twenty minutes past one o'clock, a man came into view bringing with him three horses, one of which, carrying an empty pack-saddle on its back, was the animal he was to take away. He had no difficulty in recognising the prisoner as the man who had brought him the horse. On being asked what he did with the animal after he had received it, he informed the Court that he took it back to the Warrego River, where it was afterwards seized by the police, with the pack-saddle which had been reposing on a shelf in his store ever since he had brought it home. Try how he would to do so, Perkins could not shake his assertion that I was the man who had handed him the horse.

The Government Analyst was then recalled and asked certain questions regarding the pack-saddle before mentioned. He stated that he had examined it carefully and discovered on both sides large stains, which he unhesitatingly declared to be blood, but whether the blood on the coat cuff and that on the pack-saddle were identical he could not decide. Again Perkins was to the fore, and endeavoured to prove that the marks upon the saddle might have been there prior to the ride that night. But I could see with half an eye that the Court had counted this as another point against me. The evidence of the Government Analyst concluded the hearing, and the Prosecutor thereupon asked the Court to commit me for trial. Perkins followed, and submitted that there was not sufficient evidence before the Bench to warrant them in doing anything of the sort.   It was a forcible speech but quite useless, for after a brief consultation the verdict was, 'committed for trial at the next criminal sessions to be held in Marksworth.'

I was then removed and conducted back to my cell.

How I got through the rest of that miserable day I cannot remember.   I believe I spent it cursing myself and the day I was born.   Oh, what a pitiful fool I had been!   If only I had listened to advice and had had nothing to do with Whispering Pete, what a different fate might have been mine.   Even now it was possible for me to put myself right by giving evidence against him.   But bad as my position was I could not save myself by doing that, and so I knew I must take the consequences whatever they might be.

All that afternoon and evening I sat with my head on my hands, thinking and wondering what Sheilah and her father would believe in the face of the evidence against me.   They would see that I had perjured myself to them that night when I swore I had had nothing to do with Jarman's disappearance.   What their feelings would be now seemed too horrible to contemplate.

Soon after nightfall I heard a commotion in the yard, and presently the Sergeant entered my cell. He was booted and spurred as if for a journey.

'Now, my man,' he said in a very different tone to that in which he had addressed me yesterday, ' you must prepare for a long ride. We're off to Marksworth at once. I've got an old horse for you, and I'll make it all as easy as I possibly can — provided you give no trouble, and don't make any attempt at escape.'

I was too much surprised at the suddenness of it all to do anything but assent, and so I was accordingly conducted to the yard where several horses stood ready saddled. The Sergeant had his well-known iron-grey, the trooper who was to accompany us was on another fine beast, and held the leading rein of a pack-horse in his hand, while a strong but patent safety animal was waiting for me. I mounted, and my hands were thereupon chained to the front of the saddle, the Sergeant took my reins, and we were in the act of riding out of the yard when someone ran out of the office and came towards me. It was Colin!

'Heggarstone,' he said hurriedly. 'Before you go I want to wish you good-bye and to say how sorry I am for you.'

'Thank you, Colin,' I said sincerely, more touched by his generosity than I could say, 'Tell Sheilah, will you, that I still assert my innocence, and that my every thought is of her.'

'I'll tell her,' he answered. 'You may be sure of that! Good-bye!'

Then we rode out of the yard, and down the street. Fortunately it was quite dark so our passage through the township attracted no attention. I looked at the lamp-lit windows and thought of the happy folk inside, and could have cried for very shame when I remembered that I too might have been in my own house, happy with my pretty wife, but for my own obstinate stupidity. Then we turned away from the creek, and in doing so left the houses behind us. For nearly four hours we rode steadily on in the dark—then reaching the end of a long lagoon, we stopped and prepared to camp. The trooper jumped off his horse and lit a fire, unpacked the load of the animal he led, while the Sergeant dismounted and un-fastened my handcuffs. Then I descended from the saddle and stood by the fire. As soon as the horses were hobbled and belled we had our supper, after which blankets were spread, and I laid myself down to sleep with my right hand handcuffed to the Sergeant's left wrist. Overhead the stars shone brightly, and hour after hour I lay looking up into the vault of heaven, thinking of the girl who had trusted me and whose life I had wrecked. By-and-by a lonely dingo crept down from the Ranges behind and howled at us, and then I fell asleep and did not wake till daybreak.

As soon as breakfast was finished we mounted our horses and proceeded on our way again, not to stop until mid-day, and then only for half-an-hour. All the afternoon we continued our march and all the next day—indeed, it was not till nightfall of the day following that again that we saw ahead of us the lights of Marksworth, the biggest township on our side of Queensland. Arriving there, we rode straight up to the gaol, and I was duly handed over to the Governor. A cell was allotted to me, and, thoroughly tired out, I turned into my blankets and was soon fast asleep.

Three days later the Assizes commenced,

and I learned from a warder that my case
would be the last on the list.   Mr Perkins
had obtained an eminent Brisbane barrister to
defend me, and I knew that, whatever the
result might be, I should be able to say that
I had had a good run for my money.   The
case had become widely known and had
attracted an enormous amount of attention,
so that when the morning of the trial came,
and I entered the Court, I found it crowded
to its utmost holding capacity.   The Judge sat
on the bench, clad in his robes and wig —
the barristers in their gowns and wigs occupied
their usual positions.   But though I looked
along the rows of staring people for the
face of someone I knew, I could see nobody.
Then my heart gave a great leap, for in the
front row of the gallery, heavily veiled, sat
Sheilah and her father.   I was just going to
make a sign to show that I saw her—when the
door of the dock opened again, *and who should
be ushered in than Whispering Pete.*   My
astonishment may be imagined.   I had
thought him thousands of miles away by
this time, and had as little counted on seeing
him as of having the Wandering Jew in
the dock beside me.   He was looking very
ill; his face was pinched and haggard, and

his eyes were ringed with dark circles. He bowed gravely to the Court, and then coolly shook hands with me. As he did so the work of empannelling the jury commenced, and when this had been satisfactorily accomplished, and we had both been charged and pleaded not guilty, the trial commenced. In its early stages it differed but little from the magistrate's examination, save for the wrangling and disputing that went on between the barristers. A man who had seen me ride The Unknown in the race gave evidence, followed by the individual who had met us with Jarman on the road to Pete's house, the person who had heard the cry came next, then Pete's housekeeper, and the incident of the tablecloth, after which my father, who looked in even worse health than at the magisterial examination, gave his evidence in more than his usual irritable fashion. Betty and the incident of my clothes, the Government Analyst, and the selector who had taken the horse from me followed in due order. The latter's complexion turned a sort of pea green when he was confronted with Pete. After that the Government Analyst deposed to the finding of the blood upon the pack-saddle.

When he left the box a sensation was caused by the appearance of the owner of the horse Gaybird. In answer to questions put to him he described the clever way in which the robbery of his famous horse had been accomplished. His stud groom and stable boys, it appeared, had been drugged, and the horse, with his feet swathed in flannel bandages, had been ridden out of the loose box between two and three in the morning. A blacksmith's shop was next visited and broken into, and the forge fire lit. The horse had then been re-shod all round, the only difference being that the plates were put on backwards. The result of this was that when the police thought they were following the tracks, he had in reality been going in an exactly opposite direction. That was the last he saw of the animal until he heard that he had been discovered by the Queensland police on the Warrego River, and he had gone up to identify him. Some spirited cross-examination followed, but without doing either of us very much good. The witness then stepped from the box and a Sergeant of Police took his place.

The Crown Prosecutor glanced at his notes and prepared to question him.

'On Thursday of last week, the day following the examination of one of the prisoners before the magistrates at Barranda, you received certain information, and on the strength of it you left Marksworth with another trooper and a black tracker. In what direction did you proceed?'

'To the pool known as the Blackfellow's Well, on the old Barranda road,' was the reply.

My heart turned to ice—a deadly cold sweat broke out all over me. What was coming now?

'Having arrived there, what did you do?'

'I dragged the well.'

'And what did you find?'

'A workman's shovel.'

The Crown Prosecutor took up a shovel from a heap of articles lying upon the table before him and handed it to the witness, who examined it.

'Is that what you found?'

'Yes! It is!'

'How do you recognise it?'

'By the brand upon the handle.'

'Very good. Now step down for one moment.'

The Sergeant did as he was ordered, and Timothy Cleary was called and took his place in the box. When he had been sworn, the Crown Prosecutor looked at him for a moment, and the examination proceeded as follows,—

Crown Prosecutor.—' You describe yourself as a station hand. Were you ever in the employ of either of the prisoners?'

Witness.—' I was!'

Crown Prosecutor.—' Which one?'

Witness.—' Mr Dempster.'

Crown Prosecutor.—' When, and for how long?'

Witness.—' It's difficult reckoning, sir, but 'twas in October two years back I went to him, and 'twas three months come next Tuesday that I left.'

Crown Prosecutor.—' Very good. Now take this shovel in your hand and examine it carefully. Have you ever seen it before?'

Witness.—' Many's the time, sir!'

Crown Prosecutor.—' Whose property was it when you knew it?'

Witness.—' Sure, it belonged to Mr Pete!'

Crown Prosecutor.—' The elder prisoner you mean—Peter Dempster. You are on your oath, remember, and you swear to this?'

Witness.—' I do, it's the truth sure I'm telling ye, sir, if it's my last word.'

Crown Prosecutor.—' Never mind your last word. Tell me this: How is it that you are so certain that this particular shovel was the prisoner's property?'

Witness.—'Because of the brand on the handle, and the burn just above the blade, sir! I put both on meself.'

Crown Prosecutor.—'Acting on the elder prisoner's instruction, of course?'

Witness.—'Of course, sir!'

Crown Prosecutor.—'That will do. I have done with you.'

Our barristers immediately began to cross-examine, but elicited nothing of any importance.

The Inspector of Brands was next called and sworn. His evidence was to the effect that the brand upon the shovel was that registered in the elder prisoner's name, and after our counsel had stated that he had no desire to cross-examine him he withdrew, and the Sergeant of Police who had found the implement was recalled.

He informed the Court that after discovering the shovel in question in the well, he had instituted a thorough and careful search of the locality. The result was that a rock on the hillside showed signs of having been tampered with and moved from its original position. This struck him as being curious, so he had it cleared away altogether. He then discovered that under where it had stood a large hole had been dug.

Here the excitement in Court became intense. I dared not look to right or left but stood staring straight before me at the Judge upon the bench.

'And having rolled away the stone, pray tell me what you found in that hole?' the Crown Prosecutor continued in the same remorseless voice.

'I found the decomposed body of a man sir!'

Great sensation in Court.

'And when you had made this alarming discovery, what did you do?' asked the Prosecutor.

'I brought it into Marksworth as quickly as possible.'

'Have you been able to discover whose body it was?'

'At the Coroner's inquest it was proved to be that of Jarman!'

'How was that proved?'

'By means of certain cards in a case,' the man answered, 'the name on the linen, certain letters in the pockets, and the inscription inside the cover of the watch.'

The witness then stepped down, and certain other people, strangers to me, were called. They affirmed that they had seen and identified the body as that of the Sydney detective, James Jarman.

Only one more witness remained to be examined, and he was now called. He informed the Court that he was a swagman, and that, on the night in question, he was camped near the main track on the outskirts of Barranda township. About a quarter past twelve o'clock, as nearly as he could fix it, he was awakened by the sound of horses approaching him at a smart pace. There was sufficient light for him to see that it was a man riding one horse and leading two others. The pack-horse on the right was loaded in the usual way; that on the left had a bulky package upon his back, and what looked very much like a shovel fastened to the top of it. On being asked by our counsel how he knew all this, he stated that he was lying under a tree scarcely ten yards distant from where the man passed. He could not say that he would know the rider again.

A doctor having given evidence as to the manner in which death had been caused, the case for the prosecution was at an end. For the defence a number of witnesses were called, particularly as to my character, and an attempt was made to prove that it was a matter of impossibility for me to have ridden from Barranda by the Blackfellow's Well track, dug the grave, buried the body, delivered up the horse, and reached the cattle camp at the time I did. Both our counsels made eloquent speeches, and just as dusk was falling, the Judge began his summing up. He drew the particular attention of the jury to the way in which all the circumstances of the case dovetailed into one another. The murdered man was at the house for the express purpose of arresting the prisoners on a charge of horse-stealing; he had last been seen alive by the woman who acted as housekeeper to the elder prisoner when he was sitting in that prisoner's dining-room. That was about a quarter past ten o'clock. It must be remembered by the jury, His Honour pointed out, that the younger prisoner, Heggarstone, was not present on the last occasion that she entered the room. From ten o'clock to ten-thirty it had been proved that he was in his father's house, evidently the worse for liquor. It would probably have taken him fully ten minutes in the state he was then in to walk back to the elder prisoner's house, which would bring it up to the time when another witness heard, or, more strictly speaking, thought he heard a scream come from the house. Then there were the two particulars about the burning of the tablecloth which had been used that night to be carefully considered, also the stain upon the cuff of the younger prisoner's coat, which he had gone back to his father's house to change at half-past eleven o'clock. Then it must be noted that at or about a quarter-past twelve o'clock a man was seen by another witness riding swiftly from the township on one horse, leading two others, one of which carried a peculiarly shaped burden with a shovel strapped upon it. At one-twenty, or thereabouts, the younger prisoner was met by another witness and relieved of one horse. That horse turned out to be stolen, by whom His Honour could not say, but without a doubt with the elder prisoner's knowledge and sanction. It was necessary for him to point out that there were two other cases on record against the prisoner Dempster of horse and cattle stealing in Queensland and one in the Colony of New South Wales. For each he had suffered terms of imprisonment. The police had obtained possession of the horse and pack-saddle, and the latter was found to be stained with blood. Since that time the police had discovered the shovel, marked with the prisoner's brand, at the bottom of the well near where the horse was handed over to the selector from the Warrego River; also the body of the murdered man buried beneath a rock on the hillside. The identification had been complete. In conclusion, he would draw their attention to the fact that there was a third man concerned in the case who had not yet been brought to justice, but who, doubtless, soon would be. It only remained for him to caution the jury to carefully weigh the evidence that had been submitted to them, giving the prisoners the benefit of every doubt that existed in their minds, and then to ask them to bring in a verdict in accordance with those beliefs.

When he had finished his address, the jury filed out of their box and left the Court, the Judge vanished into an adjoining room, and, amid a buzz of conversation, we were led to cells in the rear of the building. The heat was intense, and in the the interval of waiting, which was less than a quarter-of-an-hour, I seemed to live my whole life over again. God help me, what a wretched man I was! Then we were called back to our places; the Judge entered, and silence was demanded. Next moment the jury filed in again. The foreman, I remember, was a little bald-headed fellow, in a long black coat, and wore spectacles. In reply to the usual questions by the Judge's associate, he stated that he and his colleagues had arrived at a decision.

'Do you find the prisoners guilty or not guilty?'

There was such a silence in the Court that you could have heard a pin drop as we waited for his answer.

It seemed years in coming. Then the foreman said,—

'We find both prisoners guilty. The younger, however, we strongly recommend to mercy, believing him to have been intoxicated at the time and under the influence of the elder.'

A little moan came from the gallery—followed by a cry of 'Silence in the Court.' Then came the solemn question,—

'Prisoners at the bar, have you anything to say why sentence should not be pronounced against you?'

Pete went to the front of the dock, and I

thought he was going to give an explanation which would have saved me; but he only licked his thin lips and said,—

'I have nothing at all to say, Your Honour.'

I followed his example, with the addition that I reiterated my innocence.

Then the Judge turned to me and said,—

'James Heggarstone, you have been found guilty of complicity in the murder of James Jarman. You have had the benefit of the advice of a learned counsel, and you have had a fair trial. The jury, who have carefullly weighed the evidence submitted to them, have recommended you to mercy, so nothing remains for me now but to pass sentence upon you.' (Here he glanced at a paper before him.) 'The sentence of the Court, therefore, is that you suffer penal servitude for the remainder of the term of your ·natural life.'

I murmured something in reply—what I could not tell you. Just as I did so there was the sound of a heavy fall at the back of the Court, and I looked round to see two policemen carrying my father out. Then the Judge fumbled about among his papers once more, and finally took up the awful black cap, and placed it upon his head. Then he turned to Pete, who was leaning quietly on the rail, and said,—

'Peter Dempster, you have been found guilty of the cruel murder of the man James Jarman, and with that verdict I most fully concur. Of the motive for the crime I say nothing, but the sentence of this Court is that you be taken back to the place whence you came, and there be hanged by the neck until you are dead. And may God have mercy on your soul!'

While the Judge was speaking Pete did not move a muscle of his face, but looked at him just as usual, and when he had finished, said as quietly as usual,—

'I thank Your Honour.'

After that we were led away.

CHAPTER XI

HOW I ESCAPED

I AM not going to attempt to furnish you with a description of my sensations during the first fortnight of my imprisonment. It would be quite impossible to give you any adequate idea of them. I believe for the greater part of the time I was on the verge of madness, one moment buoyed up with hope that Pete, seeing his own inevitable doom approaching, would make confession of my innocence, and the next hurled down into the depths lest he should not do it at all, and so leave me, an innocent man, to suffer undeserved punishment for the remainder of my natural existence. The day of his execution was drawing closer, and with every moment my anxiety was growing more and more unbearable. As if to make it harder, by the rules of the prison I could not appeal to him in any way. Of Sheilah I dared not think at all, and by the same token I could only speculate what had happened to my father.

One morning, however, I was destined to been enlightened on two of these subjects. The Governor, going his rounds, stopped at my cell, and when I saw him I dropped the work upon which I had been engaged and stood at attention.

'Prisoner,' he said, 'you have this morning addressed a letter to me asking if the condemned man Dempster has made any confession of your innocence. In reply I have some news to give you which I fear will greatly distress you. Dempster died suddenly this morning of aneurism of the heart, leaving no confession of any kind.'

'Dead!' I cried, hardly able to believe my ears. 'And left no confession. Then I am ruined indeed! I shall have to spend my life in prison and I am an innocent man.'

With that I fell back on my bed-place and fainted away. When I recovered, the Governor was still with me. But his face was less stern than it had been.

'My man,' he said, 'if you are innocent, as you say, your case is indeed a hard one. But you must prepare yourself for some more sad news, which I think it my duty to communicate to you.'

I looked up at him with a white face. If the truth must be known, I feared some misfortune had befallen Sheilah.

'What is it, sir?' I whispered, almost afraid to speak.

'I have to tell you that your father is also dead,' he answered; 'he was seized with a stroke of paralysis in Court and lingered until this morning, when he passed quietly away.'

Strange though it may appear, a feeling of positive relief seized me when I heard this last piece of news. I had so dreaded hearing that something had befallen Sheilah that the news of my father's death failed to affect me as keenly as it would have done at any other time. Perhaps the calmness with which I received it struck the Governor as extraordinary, for he looked at me in a curious fashion, and then, with a few brief words of advice, to which I hardly listened, left the cell. When he had gone I had plenty of leisure to think over my position, and my consternation was boundless. Now that Pete was dead, and the One-eyed Doctor could not be found, my innocence might never be proved, and in that case I should have to remain a prisoner at least for thirteen years. Pete was dead, my father was dead! The words seemed to ring in my head like a passing knell. Pete was dead, my father was dead, and I—well, I was buried alive.

According to custom I was to remain at Marksworth Gaol for a month and then be transferred for the balance of my term to Burowie Convict Prison, in the township of that name, a hundred miles distant, and in the opposite direction to Barranda. So for the rest of that month I fretted on, doing the work set me almost unconsciously, dreaming all the time of my wife and the beautiful free world outside that I was not to see, save on my journey between the gaols, for thirteen long years. The mere thought of such captivity was enough to kill any man, especially one born and bred in the bush as I had been.

At last the day, long looked for, came for me to change gaols. It was scorchingly hot, and for this reason our departure was delayed till the cool of the evening. About seven o'clock I and two more prisoners were paraded in the central yard. Our guard, consisting of a sergeant and four troopers, well mounted and equipped, paraded with us, leading the three horses which were to carry us to our destination. They were not bad looking beasts, the horses I mean, but nothing like as good as those ridden by our guards. When all was ready we were ordered to mount, and having done so our hands were manacled behind us. Then the sergeant in charge taking the lead, we started off, skirted the town and the common, and at last entered the scrub.

Throughout the journey my mind was occupied, almost without cessation, endeavouring to find an opportunity to escape. But not one presented itself. Next morning we were on our way again by the time the sun was above the horizon, jogging quietly through the scrub. And now I come to recall it, I think that was the hottest day's ride I ever remember. Little by little, however, the sun sank below the tree-tops, and at last, when we had arrived at a suitable spot, the sergeant called a halt. The troopers immediately dismounted, and we were told to follow their example. While the sergeant stood guard over us, two men unharnessed the horses and turned them loose, and the other two set about preparing the camp. Suddenly, like a flash, I saw my opportunity. The sergeant's horse, the best of the whole lot, a well-bred young chestnut, had not been hobbled, and was grazing bare-backed, with his bridle still on, a short distance from the others. Thinking all was safe, the sergeant had unfastened my handcuffs for a moment to give my arms a rest. I leaned idly against a tree, keeping my eye all the time fixed upon the horse. Then suddenly I called out at the top of my voice, leaping away as I spoke.

'Great Scott, sergeant, look out for that snake!'

He jumped as if a dynamite cartridge had been exploded under his feet, and, while he was turning to look for the snake, I made a rush as hard as I could for the spot where his horse was standing. In less time than it takes to tell I had reached him, sprung upon his back, driven my heels into his sides, and was off across the plain at a racing gallop. When we had gone about fifty paces a carbine cracked in the air; but I was going too fast to be any sort of a mark for a bullet, so that did not trouble me very much. The shot, however, had one good effect; fast as my horse had hitherto been travelling, he now went even faster. Across the little open plain we dashed, into the thick scrub timber on the other side, and just as we did so I looked behind me. Short as the warning had been, two troopers were already scrambling into their saddles. Keeping well to the left, and having by this time secured the reins that at first had been flying loose about his head, I set the horse going in downright earnest. The ground was broken and by no means safe for galloping, but I trusted to be able to keep my pursuers at a distance until it was thoroughly dark, when I knew I should stand an admirable chance of giving them the slip altogether. As I left the timber, and emerged on to another bit of plain, I saw them descending the ridge behind me. What was worse, they had evidently cut a corner somehow, for now they were not more than a couple of hundred yards distant. My mind, however, was fully made up. I would risk anything, even my life, rather than be captured. If they came up with me, I was determined to fight to the death.

Once more I reached the security of the timber, but this time it was all down hill—

broken ground, strewn here and there with big rocks, and the trunks of fallen trees. But if it had been paved with razor blades I believe I should have gone down it just as fast—for could I not hear the rattle of stones and the shouts of the men behind me. Suddenly my horse stuck his forelegs out and stiffened his whole body, and experience told me he had scented danger ahead. I looked over his ears, and there, straight before me, in the half dark, was a dry water-course, stretching away as far as I could see to right and left. In front it was at least thirty feet wide and sixty feet deep—a formidable jump, even on the best steeplechaser living. What was I to do? If I turned to the right or left, the men behind me would certainly head me off and capture me. If I went back up the hill I should come face to face with them; while, if I jumped, I might break my neck and so end my flight for good and all. But one thing was certain, to remain where I was meant certain capture, so at any cost I made up my mind to attempt the leap. Taking my horse by the head, I turned him round and rode him a little way up the hill. As I did so the troopers came into view, riding helter skelter, and making certain they had got me. The nearest was not more than half a dozen lengths or so from me, when I turned my animal's head down hill again.

'It's no good, Heggarstone,' he shouted, as he saw the ravine ahead. 'You can't escape, so throw up your hands.'

'Can't I,' I cried, and digging my heels into my horse's side, I set him going again at his top speed. He tried to pull off the jump, but it was no use, I'd got him too tight by the head for that, and I wouldn't let him budge an inch. He tried to stop, but I shouted at him and forced him to go on. So, seeing that there was nothing for it but to jump, he made a dash forward, gathered his legs well under him, and went at it like a shot out of a gun. With a snort he sprang into the air. I heard the little stones he dislodged go tinkling down to the bottom of the ravine, and next moment he had landed with a scramble on the opposite bank. It was a wonderful leap, and I thanked God from the bottom of my heart that I was safely over. As I reached terra firma, I turned and looked round. The two troopers had pulled their horses up and were standing watching me. One of them was raising his carbine, so I did not stop, but waved my hand to them and disappeared into the scrub. In ten minutes I had left them far behind me, and by the time darkness had fallen was far beyond their reach.

But though I had come so well out of my scrape, I was not safe yet by any manner of means. After spelling my horse alongside a pretty little creek for half-an-hour, I mounted him again, and set off in the direction I knew Barranda to lie. About nine o'clock the moon rose, and by her rays I was able to pick my path quite comfortably. I had fully planned my movements by this time. Come what might, I was going to make my way back to the township and see Sheilah once more, if only for the last time. If she cast me off and refused to have anything more to do with me—well, then, God help me, I would either kill myself or give myself up to the police and go back to serve my sentence with the additional punishment for escape, whatever it might be.

All that night I made my way through the scrub, keeping my eyes wide open for chance travellers' camps or station homesteads. Throughout the next day I lay hidden in a cave in the Ranges, hobbling my horse with his reins, so that he could not stray very far. Unfortunately I had nothing to eat, and by nightfall I was literally starving. As soon as it was dark I went on again, still keeping a constant watch about me. Towards midnight it seemed that I was on a definite track, and presently this supposition became a certainty. I could distinctly see wheel marks, and, for this reason, I knew I must be approaching a habitation of some sort. Then the outlines of a fence hove in sight, and after a little while the white roofs of buildings, glistening in the moonlight. It was a station ; and, if I might judge by the number of huts and outhouses, a big one. Now, I told myself, if only I could get into the kitchen without exciting attention, I might be able to satisfy my hunger, and, per- haps, obtain a few provisions to carry along with me. Accordingly I got off my horse, and tied him carefully to the fence ; then, stealthily as a thieving dingo, crept across the small paddock towards the building I had settled in my own mind was the kitchen. Every moment I expected some dog to bark and give the alarm, but all was quiet as the grave. I reached the hut, and crept round it, looking in at the side window to see if anyone slept there. I could not, however, distinguish a sign, so I went back to the door and turned the handle. It opened, and I crept in. Yes! I was right. It was the kitchen, and a fire was still glimmering on the hearth. A big, old-fashioned meat safe stood along one wall, and to this I made my way. A box of matches lay on the table, and having struck one I shaded it with my hand and commenced to explore. Cooked meat there was in abundance, and a loaf and a half of bread, which I took, with a knife I discovered in a box upon the dresser. Then out again I crept, softly closing the door behind me. A minute later I was back with my horse. Before unhitching him I had a good feed, and then stowed away the rest of my provender in my pockets. What a meal that was—never before had bread and meat tasted so good. Then, mounting and gathering up my reins, I went on again—to lie hidden all the day following and the day after that. in each case resuming my journey immediately the stars appeared. So far I had been fortunate almost beyond my expectations, but the nearer I approached the township the more afraid I became of being seen. At length, by the lay of the country, and by numerous land marks familiar to me from my youth up, I knew I could not be more than fifteen miles from my home; and accordingly I started that night almost at dusk, resolved to leave my horse in a bit of thick scrub, near where Sheilah had met with her accident the previous year, and to approach the house on foot. Reaching the timber in question, I accordingly turned my horse loose, and, after a short rest, made my way towards the homestead, which was now not more than three miles distant. Just as I reached it I heard a clock in the kitchen strike ten.

Little by little, taking infinite pains not to make a noise, I made my way along the garden fence, and then, crawling through it, went on under the old familiar pepper-trees into the verandah. A light was burning in the sitting-room, and when I was near enough, I craned my neck and looked inside. Sheilah, my wife, was there alone. She was sitting in her father's arm-chair, knitting—though, at the moment that I looked, her work lay in her lap, and she was staring into the empty fireplace. Her face was just as beautiful as ever—but, oh, so worn and sad. While I watched her she heaved a great sigh, and I saw large tears rise in her eyes. Something seemed to tell me that she was thinking of me, so creeping closer to the window I rapped softly with my fingers upon the pane. Instantly she sprang to her feet and ran to the door; another minute and she was in the verandah and in my arms.

'Oh, Jim, Jim! my husband! my dear, dear boy!' she whispered again and again. 'Thank God you have come back to me once more.'

The tears were streaming down my cheeks, and my heart was beating like a wheat flail against my ribs, but I had the presence of mind to draw her into the house and shut the door as quickly as possible. Then I disengaged myself from her arms and looked at her.

'Sheilah,' I said, 'you should not receive me in this fashion. I am not worthy.'

'Hush! hush!' she cried; 'you must never say that to me. Jim, to me you are innocent; let the world say what it will. I am convinced you did not do it.'

'But, Sheilah, I am not as innocent as you think. No, no! Do not look so scared. I did not kill the man, but I told you a lie when I said that I knew nothing of his death. I did know something about it, for I saw him murdered — but I could not say so, or I must have betrayed another man. I had sworn to Pete that I would not reveal what I had seen. So my lips were tied.'

'My own dear husband,' she said, looking up into my face, and then led the way towards the sitting-room, 'I have never thought you guilty. But come in here now—I must not let you be seen. Your escape is known to the police, and they were here looking for you only this afternoon.'

'Where is your father, Sheilah?'

'He has gone up to the township to attend a meeting of the Presbyterian Church. He may be back at any moment. First you must change your clothes. Go in there,' and as she spoke she opened the door of her own bedroom. 'You will find a suit hanging in the cupboard. While you are doing that, I will prepare a meal for you.'

I did not stop to ask how she had come to prepare for me in this way, but went into the room and changed my things as I was told to do. That done, and having folded the other hateful garments up and hidden them on the top of the cupboard, I rejoined her in the sitting-room. By this time she had a meal spread on the table for me, but I did not want to eat until I had told her the whole history of my trouble from beginning to end, without keeping anything back.

'And now, Sheilah,' I said, in conclusion of my narrative, 'Whispering Pete is dead.

And what is worse, he died without exonerating me. Therefore, if I am caught, I shall have to go back to gaol again and serve my sentence to the bitter end.'

'But you must not be caught. I have taken steps to ensure your safety. As soon as you have eaten your meal you must start again. I have a saddle-horse and pack-horse ready in the stable—they have been there every night since you left here. You must take them, cross the border near Engonia, and set off by a roundabout route marked on this map for Newcastle—arriving there, you will go to this address (here she gave me a slip of paper which I deposited in my pocket) and interview the captain of the ship named upon it. I have got a friend whom I can trust implicitly to arrange it all. The captain will give you a passage to Valparaiso, and three hundred pounds when you land there. You can either settle in Chili or the South Sea Islands as you think best. In either case, when a year has elapsed, if you will let me know where you are I will join you. In the meantime, I am going to set to work to find this One-eyed Doctor, Finnan, and to prove your innocence.'

'Sheilah!' I cried, 'what can I say to you?'

'Say nothing, Jim, but do as I tell you.

Remember your wife believes in you, whatever the world may say. So be brave and cautious for my sake.'

'And, Sheilah, you forgive me for that lie I told you? Oh! my darling, what misery my foolish obstinacy has brought upon us all—my father included.'

'But it will all end well yet, Jim; only you must do exactly as I tell you!'

At that moment my ear caught the sound of a footstep on the path. Sheilah heard it as soon as I did, and cried,—

'Jim, somebody is coming; you must hide. In here at once!'

She led the way to her own room, and made me go inside. A moment later I heard someone enter the room I had just quitted.

'Colin,' cried Sheilah, trying to speak in her natural voice, 'what on earth brings you down here at this time of night?'

'I have come to warn you, Sheilah,' said her cousin, 'that we have received information that your husband is on his way here. You know, don't you, that if he is discovered he will be at once arrested and taken back?'

'You would not arrest him, Colin, would you?' Sheilah asked, in agonised tones. 'Surely you could not be so cruel to me!'

Colin had evidenly been studying her face.

'I'm afraid I should fail in my duty for your sake, Sheilah,' he said, after a moment's pause. But, my cousin, you know more than you are telling me. Sheilah! I see it all; Jim is here!'

Sheilah must have felt that she could trust him, for she answered,—

'You are right. He is here. Colin, you will not act against him?'

'Have I not told you I shall not! But remember, Sheilah, this will cost me my position. I shall send in my resignation to-morrow.'

At this I walked out, and Colin stared; but did not say that he was glad to see me.

'Jim,' my wife said, 'everything is prepared; you must go. Colin is your friend, you can trust him. Now come. Every moment you are here increases your danger.'

I went over to Colin McLeod and looked him in the face.

'McLeod,' I said, 'you are acting the part of a brave and true man. God bless you for it. Tell me one thing, do you believe me guilty of the charge upon which I was con-victed?'

'No! I do not,' he answered; 'if I did I should not be helping you now.'

'Then I'll ask you to shake hands with me.'

We shook hands; and, after that, without another word, I followed Sheilah into the darkness. As she had said, two horses stood saddled and ready in the stockyard. I led them out, and, having done so, took Sheilah in my arms.

'My wife,' I said, 'my Sheilah, what a wonderful and beautiful faith is yours! Who else would have believed in me as you have done, through good and ill report!'

'It is because I love you so, and because I know you better than you know yourself that I believe in you as I do,' she answered. 'Now, Jim, darling, good-bye. Let me know what happens to you. Write, not only before you leave Australia, but when you arrive in Chili; and, for my sake, be careful. May the good God be with you and keep you safe for me. Good-bye—oh, Jim, Jim, good-bye.'

I kissed her sweet, upturned face again and again, and then, tearing myself away from her, passed through the slip panels, which she had let down for me, and with a last wave of my hand rode off into the dark night, feeling that

I had left what was more than my life behind me.

Passing through old McLeod's paddock I made my way carefully along the creek side to the old ford — the place where I had fought Colin McLeod one memorable evening, and where I had spent that awful night after I had lied to Sheilah about Jarman's death and she had believed and kissed me before them all. Before I went down the steep bank to the water's edge I checked my horse and looked back across the paddocks to where I could just distinguish the outline of the house that sheltered the woman I loved. How much had happened and how terrible had been my life since I had last stood in this place and had gazed in the same direction. Then, turning my eyes across the stream, I made out the house I had built with such pride and loving care; the home to which I was to have brought my wife after the wedding that had ended so disastrously. There it stood, dark and forlorn, the very picture of loneliness, a grave of disappointed hopes if ever there was one. The garden was straggling and overgrown, the building itself already cried aloud for attention. Almost unconscious of my actions, I crossed

the ford and rode up to within a few yards
of it, thinking of the happy days I had
spent in building it, of the good resolutions
I had then formed, and the way in which I
had afterwards failed in the trust reposed in
me. In the darkness and silence of the
night the place seemed haunted with phantoms
of the past. I almost fancied I could see my
father in one corner, and Pete from another,
watching me, the outlaw, as I sat in my
saddle under the big Gum Tree, gazing at
what might once have been the very centre
of all that could have made life beautiful.
At last, saddened almost to the verge of
despair, I urged my horse forward and quitted
the spot, heaving a heavy sigh as I did so
for *auld lang syne*, and all the happiness
that might have been my portion had I
only shunned Pete at the commencement of
our acquaintance instead of trusting him
and believing in him against my better
judgment. Now, however, that it was all
over and done with, there was nothing for
it but for me to eat my bread of sorrow
and drink my water of affliction alone. In
the words of the old saying, I had made
my bed, and now it was my portion to ' lie
upon it.

Leaving the house, I made my way by a path, which I had good reason to know as well as any man living, in the direction of my old home. Like the other house it was quite dark. Not a light shone from the windows, though instinctively I turned towards those of the dining‑room where my father had been wont to sit, half expecting to see one there. For my own part I did not know whether there was anyone still living in the house. My father was dead, I was cut off from the society of the living, Betty might be dead, too, for all I knew to the contrary. Repressing a groan, I turned my horse's head and set off through the scrub in the direction Sheilah had advised me to follow.

By the time the sun rose next morning I had put upwards of thirty miles between myself and Barranda township. I had travelled as quickly as possible in order that I might have more time to lay by later on, for I was determined to push on at night and to camp during the day. I had two reasons for this decision. In the first place, I wanted to give my beard a chance of growing, in order that my appearance might be altered as much as possible, and in the second, because I knew that in a district where I was so well known the chances would be a thousand to one that someone would recognise me in the daylight, and thus lead up to my recapture. For the first two or three days, however, complete success crowned my efforts. I was fortunate enough to be able to make my way across country each night without atrracting atten-tion. But a serious fright was saving up for me.

On the third day after I had said good-bye to Sheilah and Barranda township, I found myself leaving the Mallee scrub and entering more open country. Here I did not like to attract attention by camp-ing during the day. Accordingly I made up my mind to risk meeting anyone who might know me, and, saddling my horse, started down the track. It was a warm morning, and seeing the amount of work that still lay before him, I did not push my horse too hard. I therefore jogged easily along, smoking my pipe, and thinking of Sheilah, my pretty wife, and of the old life I had left behind me. For upwards of an hour I had been following a faint track, which was now fast developing into a well-defined road. A little later I heard behind me the sound of a couple of horses coming along at a slow, swinging canter. For the reason that I was only travelling at a walk they soon caught me up, when I discovered that the new‑comer was a smart, active, fresh‑complexioned young fellow, obviously an Englishman, mounted on a neat bay and leading a clever‑looking grey pack-horse beside him.

'Good morning,' he said, as he drew up alongside me. 'Pretty warm, ain't it? Travelling far?'

In case I should be questioned I had already decided upon the sort of answer I would return.

'I'm thinking of turning off after the next township,' I said, 'and following the river down till I strike the track for Bourke.' Then reflecting that if he were an experienced bushman he would find something wrong in this, I hastened to add, 'I should have gone in higher up, I know, and followed the coach road along the foot of the Ranges, but they say the country thereabouts is all burnt up and travelling is next door to an impossibility.'

'That is so,' he answered. 'I've come

over the border myself, and had a pretty rough time of it out towards the Warrego. Are you droving?'

'Going down for a mob to take out to the Diamintina,' I answered. 'One of Blake & Furley's of Callington Plains.'

He shook his head.

'I don't know them,' he said. 'I'm next door to a new chum myself; been out on the Balloo best part of three years. Now, however, I'm going to take a jolly good holiday.'

For an hour or so we jogged on side by side, talking of horses, cattle, sheep, and half a hundred other things. Then the township came into view, and nothing would please my new friend but we must pull up at the grog shanty and take a drink. I would have made an excuse and have said good-bye to him, but he would not hear of such a thing. Accordingly, very loth, but unable to persist in my refusal for fear of exciting his suspicions, I consented and we pulled up at the Drover's Arms, as the shanty was called, and having made our horses fast to the rail outside, went in to the bar. There were two or three other men of the usual bar loafer stamp present at the time, and according to bush custom they were invited to join us in our refreshment. To my horror, as we were satisfying their curiosity as to whence we had come and whither we were going, and what the track was like further up, a police trooper entered and called for a nobbler of whiskey.

'How are you, Sergeant?' asked one of the loafers with well simulated interest. 'Any news to-day of the man you're looking for?'

The Sergeant shook his head.

'Not yet,' he answered; 'but we'll nab him before long, never fear.'

'Who are you looking for?' inquired my companion, with sudden interest.

'For Jim Heggarstone,' replied the Sergeant; 'the man who got a lifer for being mixed up with Whispering Pete in that murder case out Barranda way in Queensland. He escaped on his way to gaol, and we were told to look out for him in this direction, as it is supposed he is making south.'

My heart seemed to stand still for a moment as he turned round and ran his eye over me. I felt that I must make some remark, but what to say that would avert suspicion I could not for the very

life of me think. At last I found my
voice.

'What is he like—this, what's his name
—Heggarfield?' I inquired, as coolly as I
knew how.

The Sergeant glanced at me again as
he answered,—

'Oh, a decent - sized sort of fellow.
About your height, or a little taller, I
should say.'

To my intense relief I was not permitted
to monopolize the great man's attention for
very long, as one of the loafers was
desirous of learning what punishment the
criminal would be likely to receive when he
was captured and taken back to gaol.

'A year in irons, most likely,' I heard
the Sergeant answer as I paid for the
drinks and, lighting my pipe, sauntered
out into the verandah, feeling ready to
drop in my anxiety to be out of the
township once more. As soon as my
companion was ready, which seemed to me
an eternity, we mounted our horses, and
waving our adieux to the loafers in the
bar, set off down the street, and in something less than a quarter - of - an - hour were
clear of the houses and bidding each other

good-bye at the spot where the three cross roads branched off. Two days later I joined a mob of fat cattle *en route* to Bourke, with whom I kept company until I reached the town. Then having sold my horse, saddle and bridle to the drover in charge, I found the railway station, purchased a ticket for Sydney, and placing myself on board the train was next day landed safe and sound in the capital. To make my way thence to Newcastle was a matter of small difficulty.

Once there, I hastened to seek out the address written on the paper Sheilah had given me. It was a nice house in a fashionable locality, and when I inquired for Captain Blake of the *Amber Crown* steamer, and gave my name as George Brown, I was told by the maid servant to walk in.

It appeared that old McLeod had once done a signal service for my new friend, which the latter had never forgotten. For this reason he was only too glad to have an opportunity of repaying his benefactor. Whether or not he knew who I was I cannot say; at any rate he said nothing to me on the subject. When I said good-bye to him I went straight off and boarded the

Amber Crown, then lying in the harbour. The following morning I wrote to Sheilah, and during the afternoon we weighed anchor; by nightfall Australia lay beneath the horizon behind us. I was free!!!

Of the voyage across the Pacific there is nothing to tell. On arrival at Valparaiso I had an interview with Captain Blake in his private cabin.

'Mr Brown,' said he, for, as I have said, that was the name I was travelling under, 'having landed you here, I have carried out half of my contract. Now I must fulfil the other half.'

As he spoke he handed me a canvas bag containing the three hundred pounds in English gold Sheilah had told me to expect. I thanked him for his kindness to me during the voyage, signed the receipt for Mr McLeod, and then went ashore. The same night I sailed aboard an island schooner bound for Tahiti, the capital of the Friendly Group, where I entered the employ of the firm for whom I am now trading here on Vakalavi.

Now, my friends, you know my curious story, and there remain but three things to tell. The One-eyed Doctor was discovered at last by Sheilah, after a tedious hunt, dying of consumption in a Melbourne slum. She nursed him, and in a moment of gratitude, with the hand of death clutching at his throat, he gave her, in the presence of a magistrate, a full and complete confession of the murder of Jarman by Whispering Pete, stating that, beyond burying the body, I had nothing whatsoever to do with it. So my innocence was established, and I was cleared before the whole world. That is the first thing. Now for the next. Your schooner to-day brought me a letter from my wife, in which she tells me that she is coming to join me by the next boat. God bless her! Her father, who is tired of Barranda, is accompanying her. That is the second! The third is that by my father's death, so the lawyers and bankers tell me, I am a rich man. This being so, I shall send in my resignation to the firm, move across to Apia, and once there, set about building a big house on the mountain side overlooking the bay. In that lovely spot, for I shall never go back to Australia now, I shall hope to begin a new life, with Sheilah for my sweet companion. There is one point, doubtless, upon which you will agree with me, and that is, try how I will, I shall never be able to make up to her for her confidence and love during the bitterest period of my life. But I'll try, God helping me, I'll try!— you may be sure of that.

And now you know why I say that I believe in and reverence the name of woman. God bless the sex, and, above all, the girl, now my wife, who was once SHEILAH McLEOD!

THE END

Colston & Coy. Limited, Printers, Edinburgh.